Animal Stories for
Eight Year Olds

Helen Paiba is known as one of the most committed, knowledgeable and acclaimed children's booksellers in Britain. For more than twenty years she owned and ran the Children's Bookshop in Muswell Hill, London, which under her guidance gained a superb reputation for its range of children's books and for the advice available to its customers.

Helen was involved with the Booksellers Association for many years and served on both its Children's Bookselling Group and the Trade Practices Committee. In 1995 she was given honorary life membership of the Booksellers Association of Great Britain and Ireland in recognition of her outstanding services to the association and to the book trade. In the same year the Children's Book Circle (sponsored by Books for Children) honoured her with the Eleanor Farjeon Award, given for distinguished service to the world of children's books.

She retired in 1995 and now lives in London.

Animal
STORIES
for Eight Year Olds

COMPILED BY HELEN PAIBA

ILLUSTRATED BY DIZ WALLIS

MACMILLAN
CHILDREN'S BOOKS

For my parents-in-law who would have enjoyed these stories. *H.P.*

First published 1998 by Macmillan Children's Books
a division of Pan Macmillan Ltd
Pan Macmillan, 20 New Wharf Road, London N1 9RR
Basingstoke and Oxford
Associated companies throughout the world
www.panmacmillan.com

ISBN 0 330 35495 7

7 9 8

A CIP catalogue record for this book is available
from the British Library.

Typeset by SX Composing DTP, Rayleigh, Essex
Printed and bound in India by
Replika Press Pvt. Ltd.

Contents

Woolly

Dick King-Smith

Snaggletooth was a caveman. He was short and strong and bow-legged and hairy, and he had a wife called Flatface.

Snaggletooth had several broken teeth that stuck out of his wide mouth, and his wife's face was indeed flat, and it isn't hard to guess why they called their small son Bat-ears.

One day Snaggletooth came rushing into their cave in high excitement.

"Guess what I've found, down by the river," he cried.

"Food, Snag?" said Flatface hopefully.

"Enough to last us for ages! A mammoth!"

"A mammoth? However will you be able to kill that?"

"I don't have to. It's dead already. Come

on!" said Snaggletooth, and he hoisted Bat-ears on to his shoulders and set off back towards the river, Flatface following.

The huge animal was lying on its side, and while his parents stood gaping at the size of it, Bat-ears climbed up on top of it.

Behind it was a very sad-looking mammoth calf. Its tail hung down straight, its ears drooped, its head was bent, the eyes half closed. It looked the picture of misery.

Oh dear, thought Bat-ears, it must be his mother who's died, and he slid down the far side of the body and stood before the youngster. It was not much taller than him.

"Hullo," he said. "I'm Bat-ears. What's your name?"

"Haven't got one," replied the little mammoth.

Bat-ears stroked the thick sandy hair with which the calf was covered.

"You're woolly," he said, "so that's what I'll call you. Come and meet my mum and dad."

Snaggletooth and Flatface were surprised when Bat-ears appeared from behind the body, followed by the calf.

Trustingly, it already rested the tip of its trunk on his shoulder.

"Look!" he cried. "This is Woolly!" but at that very moment they heard in the distance a horrible noise, a sort of mad screeching laughter, and saw a crowd of ugly spotted shapes approaching at a gallop.

"Hyenas!" said Snaggletooth. "Quick, Bat-ears, jump on my back."

But Bat-ears was already mounted. He was sitting astride Woolly, legs tucked behind the young mammoth's ears, hands gripping the thick fleece.

"Go, Woolly, go!" he squeaked, and away they all went at top speed towards the river.

The river was a very big one, and out in the middle of it was a large island. Woolly pointed his little trunk at it.

"That's a nice place," he said to Bat-ears. "No hyenas. Plenty of good food."

"How do you know?"

"We used to go there."

"We? Oh, you mean you and your . . ."

". . . mother," said Woolly in a small voice.

"Oh. But how did you get there?"

3

"We swam."

"But none of us can swim."

"You don't have to," said Woolly. "I'll carry you, like I'm doing now. Your mum can ride behind you, and your dad can hang on to my tail."

"You can forget that," said Snaggletooth, who was frightened of the water. "There's no way I'm going in that water."

But then they heard the horrid laughter again. Some of the hyenas were coming down to the river to drink.

"Quick, Snag!" said Flatface, hastily clambering up behind Bat-ears.

"Quick, Dad!" cried Bat-ears.

"Quick!" trumpeted Woolly, and as the leading hyena dashed up, Snaggletooth threw himself desperately into the water. He grabbed hold of the young mammoth's tail, and away they went.

The island, they found, was a perfect paradise. It was covered in leafy trees so that there was plenty for Woolly to eat, and living on it were many small animals for the meat-

4

eating cave-people to catch and many nestfuls of fat white sausage-shaped grubs whenever they just felt like a snack.

Soon the cave-people discovered how useful to them Woolly was to be. He found trees of crab-apple and other wild fruit and broke off branches for them, he found bushes heavy with berries, he found patches of mushrooms, and dug up delicious truffles with his little tusks. He even found a wild bees' nest, and with his trunk he pulled out the comb for them. Never had they eaten so well.

"This is the life," said Snaggletooth, his mouth full of honey. "Shall we stay here, Snag?" said Flatface.

"Can we, Dad?" said Bat-ears.

Snaggletooth had only ever lived in a cave. "Where shall we sleep?" he said.

"Under the trees," said Flatface. "The weather's lovely and warm and settled and there's masses of food."

"And we shan't be short of a drink," said Bat-ears.

The river, they soon found, was not just a protection against enemies. It was also full of fish, which Woolly caught for them.

He would dangle his trunk in the water, and when a fish swam up to investigate, he would suck so that the fish was drawn tight against his trunk-tip. Then, with a swing of his head, he would flip it out on to the bank.

He tossed out frogs too with that trunk, and shook down squirrels from bushes, and picked out eggs from birds' nests.

"Woolly!" Flatface would say. "Whatever should we do without you!"

All the same, she worried about the approach of winter. What would they do when it grew really cold, with no cave to shelter in? If only our people knew how to make fire, she thought – for once, when young, she had seen a forest ablaze, set off by a lightning strike, and she remembered the crackling of the flames, and the smoke, and above all the heat. There's plenty of dead wood on the island, she told herself, but no way to burn it.

She was wrong.

One day they were all gathered round a tree that had fallen some long time ago by the look of it. It was partly hollow, and the wood inside it was so decayed as to be as soft and dry as powder – touchwood, in fact.

Snaggletooth and Flatface were searching for grubs, and Woolly was stripping off and eating some of the remaining bark.

His appetite satisfied, he picked up a sharp piece of stick with his trunk and began to play with it, pushing it into the touchwood and twiddling it to and fro, first one way, then the other, while Bat-ears watched idly. Held in that agile trunk-tip, the stick rotated faster and faster, gradually drilling a hole in the touchwood. And then suddenly a wisp of smoke came up out of the hole!

"Look!" cried Bat-ears.

Snaggletooth and Flatface looked.

Woolly withdrew the stick.

Snaggletooth put his finger in the hole.

"Yeow!" he said. "Hot!"

Flatface grabbed a handful of dry grass.

"Go on, Woolly," she said.

Woolly twiddled some more.

"Faster! Faster!" cried Flatface, and as the smoke rose again, she began to feed the grass into the hole in the touchwood.

"Twigs. Leaves. Anything dry, quick!" she said to the others, and then it was, as Woolly's wonderful trunk twiddled on, that a tiny flicker was seen, the first little flame of the first fire ever lit on the face of the earth, not by nature, but by man.

Or rather, to be fair, by a mammoth.

Once they had become skilled in fire-making, something else happened that was to change their way of life. Up till then, cave-people had always eaten their meat raw, just like the hyenas and the cave bears and the sabre-toothed tigers.

On the island, Snaggletooth and his family gobbled down the mice or squirrels or lizards that they caught, or the frogs and fish that Woolly caught for them, not knowing that there was a much tastier way of eating them. And once again, it was Woolly who made the breakthrough.

One evening the family were sitting round a roaring fire (for the nights were growing colder) and eating a meal of fish that Woolly had caught for them, when suddenly the

mammoth picked up a fish with his trunk and dropped it into the hot embers at the edge of the blaze. The fish began to sizzle.

"Oh, Woolly," said Flatface. "Why did you do that? That's a fish wasted."

"Unless you can fish it out," said Snaggle-tooth. He laughed loudly at his own joke.

Woolly picked up a long stick and with it he moved the fish about so that first one side of it and then the other was exposed to the heat. All the while the fish sizzled and hissed, while there rose from it a smell that was quite new to all of them, a delicious smell that made their mouths water.

Then Woolly flipped the fish out on to the grass, and once it was cool enough, the cave-people each took a bite.

So it was that, thanks to a mammoth, Snaggletooth and his family became the first people on earth not only to make fire, but to discover cooking.

Not that they gave up eating meat raw on occasion, for their stomachs were strong and old habits die hard, and they would still pop such morsels as caterpillars into their mouths uncooked. But cooking, they found, made things so much nicer to eat, especially after Woolly had yet another brainwave.

One day he came back from the river's edge, carrying something he had found there. It was the shell of a big turtle. The body had been eaten by ants and other scavengers, and only the deep basin-shaped shell was left. This, once Woolly had explained things to Flatface, became the world's first cooking utensil.

The shell, in which handfuls of fat white

grubs had been put, was laid in the fire, which quickly melted the grubs into a bubbling pool of fat. Into this fat were put not only the fish but also slivers of a large tuber-shaped vegetable which Woolly had dug up with his tusks, and Flatface had sliced up with a sharp flint. So, once again thanks to the mammoth, there came about another first – fish and chips.

So, as the years passed, Woolly and his friends continued to live happily on the island in the middle of the great river. Snaggletooth had made himself a stone axe with which he chopped down trees and built a sort of house in which the family could shelter from the occasional downpour (Woolly didn't mind the rain), and they always had plenty to eat.

In fact, Flatface became quite a good cook, inventing interesting recipes like boiled squirrel with frog sauce or fried snake garnished with green caterpillar dressing.

During all those years Woolly grew big and Bat-ears grew tall and Snaggletooth grew fat.

Other cavemen living on either side of the river saw the smoke rising by day from the fires on the island and saw the flames of them by night. If the wind was in the right direction they smelled delicious strange smells and heard voices and laughter and an occasional shrill trumpeting noise. They were scared, believing the island to be haunted, and none of them, even had it been possible, would have dared set foot on it.

So, for the islanders, everything seemed to be perfect. But it wasn't, quite, as Bat-ears and Woolly overheard one day.

They had been down to the river to bathe (something that Snaggletooth and Flatface never did; in fact neither had ever in their whole lives even washed), and Bat-ears was riding home on his friend's great back. Woolly, now the owner of a magnificent pair of curving tusks, moved silently on his large cushioned feet. He stopped behind some bushes, close to the family house, to pull down the fruit with that long trunk of his. Bat-ears, a young man by now, slipped down to the ground, and at that moment heard his mother's voice.

"Snag," she was saying. "Are you happy?"

"Happy?" said Snaggletooth, rubbing his stomach, full as usual. "Of course I am. Aren't you?"

"Oh yes." said Flatface, "except for one thing."

"What's that?"

Flatface did not answer for a moment, occupied as she was with tidying her matted grey locks with a comb made from a reed-buck's shoulder blade.

Then she said, "I just wish we could have had a grandchild. I'd love to have a little granddaughter, or a little grandson."

Her husband put his hand in his mouth and fingered one of his snaggle teeth. It was loose, on account of his age, and now he pulled it out and threw it away.

"Grandchildren?" he said. "How's our Bat-ears going to manage that without a wife?"

This time Flatface made no answer, but the eavesdroppers could clearly hear the deep sad sigh she gave.

Not only was each struck by the same thought, but each knew what the other was thinking.

So it was that one morning not long after that, Snaggletooth and Flatface woke to find themselves alone on the island. Bat-ears and Woolly had disappeared!

They followed the mammoth's tracks, leading down to the river bank, but there was no sign of the pair. There was a message however. Drawn in the sand by the water's edge were two large arrows. One pointed to the distant shore, from which they had all come, so many years ago. The other pointed the reverse way, inland, towards their house.

"Oh, Snag!" cried Flatface, pointing to the first arrow. "They've gone and left us."

Snaggletooth pointed to the second arrow.

"But they'll come back," he said.

"When?"

"How do I know?"

In fact, months passed with no sign of them, until suddenly one day the two old cave-people heard a loud shout coming from the direction of the river.

"Mum! Dad!" called Bat-ears over the wide waters. "We're back!"

And as they ran down to the bank, they saw the great head of Woolly approaching, trunk curled high out of the water, Bat-ears aboard.

But then their mouths fell agape in utter amazement. For sitting behind Bat-ears was another figure, the figure, they saw, of a tow-haired cave-girl.

"Now," said Bat-ears when they had landed and the mammoth had shaken the water from his hairy sides, "let me introduce you. Mum, Dad, I want you to meet my girlfriend, Snubnose."

All that happened at the beginning of winter, and the following summer, would you believe, Snubnose had a little girl.

Bat-ears was the proudest of fathers, and Snaggletooth was quite chuffed to be a grandfather, and Flatface was utterly delighted with her granddaughter.

"She's got your ears," she said to her son, and to her daughter-in-law, "and your nose."

"And your face, Mum," said Bat-ears.

"But not your teeth, Snag," said Flatface.

Thank goodness, she thought.

All this time Woolly stood silently by, his little piggy eyes gazing affectionately down on the baby.

"What are you going to call her?" Snaggletooth asked the young couple.

"Well," said Snubnose, "Bat-ears wants to call her after his great friend, but 'Woolly' does sound a bit funny for a girl, doesn't it?"

"When she grows up," said Bat-ears, "we shall all tell her about the wonderful things her Uncle Woolly has done for us all."

He looked up at the mammoth. "Perhaps you'd like to suggest a name?" he said.

Very gently Woolly stretched out his trunk, and with the tip of it stroked the baby's head, already thickly covered in little ringlets. So fascinated was he that he hadn't been listening to what Bat-ears had said.

"She's lovely," he said dreamily.

"Oh, Woolly," said Bat-ears. "I might have known you'd pick just the right name! We'll call her Lovely."

Sid the Mosquito

Colin Thompson

Behind the trees at the end of the lawn, the pond lay hidden by overgrown bushes. The trees hung their branches down to touch the water and at the water's edge tall grass grew full of hidden flowers and butterflies. Birds nesting in the trees flashed across the water catching flies and their voices filled the air with music.

Dragonflies danced in the air like sparkling jewels unseen by anyone except the mice and birds who went to drink at the water's edge. In the pond its elf little creatures lived their secret lives. Tiny snails wriggled in the soft mud at the bottom of the pond. Water beetles and worms darted between the roots of water lilies. Beneath the top of the water, mosquito larvae hung like baby caterpillars waiting to become butterflies. Then very early one morning, before the sun was even up, they all changed into mosquitoes and flew off into the jungle of soft grass beneath the honeysuckle.

"Can I go and bite something now, Mum?" said a young mosquito called Sid.

"No, dear," said his mother.

"Oh go on, Mum," said Sid. "Everyone knows mosquitoes bite things."

"Not boys," said his mother. "Boys don't bite things, only girls do that." All Sid's sisters giggled and nudged each other and pointed.

"But what am I going to have for my breakfast if I can't bite something?" cried Sid.

"You have to suck pollen out of buttercups, you do," sneered his eldest sister, and they all giggled again.

"It's not true," said Sid with tears in his eyes, but it was. His mother tried to explain as gently as she could that boy mosquitoes and girl mosquitoes were made differently and that with his delicate mouth he just wouldn't be able to bite anything.

18

"You just go and get your head into a nice dandelion," she said.

"I'm not sucking soppy flowers," said Sid. "Everyone'll laugh at me."

"No they won't," said his mother. "Your father loved pollen. Why, he spent half his life with his head buried in bluebells."

Sid felt as if someone had played a rotten trick on him. It had been no fun wiggling around in the pond as a larva, dodging out of the way of the horrid dragonflies and the drinking dog and swimming around with his ears full of stagnant water and hedgehog spit. It had been no fun at all and the only thing that had kept him going had been the thought of biting a nice soft human leg. And now they were telling him that all he was going to get was soppy flowers.

"And keep away from the roses until you're grown up," she added. "They're much too strong for a young lad like you."

The sun climbed above the house, sending its clear light through the branches above the pond. The air grew warmer and one by one Sid's sisters all flew off to bite things. While his mother went down to the the shops to bite a greengrocer, Sid kicked his feet in the earth and sulked under a nettle all morning. There was no way he was going to put his head inside a flower and that was final. He was going to bite a human, or at least a dog. He would even settle for a small mouse but certainly not a dandelion.

The morning became the afternoon and Sid grew hungrier and hungrier. As his sisters came and went with tales of blood they had drunk from policemen's necks and sparrows' knees, Sid listened to his tummy rumble until at last he could stand it no longer.

As soon as no one was looking, he flew off to the house next door to bite a baby.

Noises and new smells floated out of the open windows. There were humans inside, laughing and talking and eating. Sid landed on the window sill and looked at their bare arms. There was a big pink juicy baby sitting on the floor sucking a sock. Sid was about to fly down to it when he noticed one of his three hundred and five sisters sitting on someone's ear. As he watched, a hand flashed through the air and squashed her. Sid turned and fled.

In next-door's garden their dog snored gently under a deck-chair and Sid decided it would be safer to start with him. He landed on the grass, tiptoed across to the sleeping animal, shut his eyes and pounced.

The next thing he knew, he was flying through the air with a sore nose and tears streaming from his eyes.

"Get out of it," growled an angry voice in the dog's fur.

"Yeah," said another, "or we'll pull your wings off."

"Yeah, that's right," said a third.

Sid sat up and shook his head. Something dark and horrible leapt out of the dog and landed in front of him. It was an angry flea with a mean look in its eye.

"Listen, sonny," it said, "that's our dog that is, so watch it. You just push off back to the buttercups where you belong."

"Yeah, push off," the third flea said again from somewhere behind the dog's left ear.

Sid crept off into the quiet heart of a big red rose bush and hid behind a sharp thorn.

He could hear the fleas all laughing but after a while the dog got up and wandered off and it was peaceful again. His nose was still very sore and he really was very hungry by then, so, forgetting his mother's advice, he stuck his tongue into the middle of a big red rose.

His mouth was filled with a million wonderful tastes. The pollen tasted like strawberry jam, caramel pudding and black cherry ice cream all rolled into one. As he wriggled his tongue around he picked up the nectar which was even more wonderful, like thick chocolate sauce and creme eggs floating in condensed milk. Of course, Sid was only a little mosquito and had never heard of chocolate or all the other delicious things. All he knew was that what he was eating was totally amazingly completely fantastic and he was feeling sick.

In no time at all, he was so full up he couldn't fly. He staggered around in the grass with a silly grin on his face and finally bumped into his mother.

"Hello, Mummy," he mumbled and fell flat

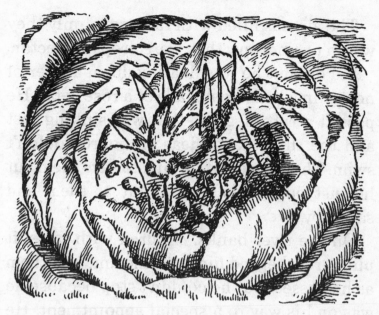

on his back. He lay there waving his legs in the air and singing a little song.

"Sidney, you've been in the rose bush, haven't you?" said his mother, pretending to be cross.

"Hello, Mummy," he said again.

"And what's happened to your nose? Have you been fighting?"

"Big flea bashed me," said Sid and fell fast asleep. Soon he was far away in the land of dreams where huge roses grew as big as flying saucers. 43

The air was filled with raindrops, only they weren't raindrops, they were drops of nectar.

Sid dreamt he was floating down a river of nectar in a little boat made of a rose petal. He passed a raft of grass that was sinking fast and the three nasty fleas on board couldn't swim. They cried out for him to save them but he just poked his tongue out at them and sailed by.

On the river banks, children with big soft pink arms begged him to come and bite them as he passed, but he couldn't stop because he was on his way to a special appointment. He dreamt that the Queen of England herself had sent him a telegram requesting his presence at Buckingham Palace where he was to bite her Majesty's left ear, and for pudding he was to have a go at all the royal corgis.

When Sid woke up, it really was raining. His mother had bitten off a piece of grass and covered him with it so only his feet sticking out of the bottom were getting wet. Like all insects everywhere he climbed up under a leaf to keep dry and sat next to an old spider, waiting for the rain to pass. The spider kept complaining that when she was a girl it was always nice and sunny and never rained at all.

By the time the sky was clear again, evening was falling and Sid's sisters began to come home. Some flew in alone, some came in twos or threes and other arrived in groups.

Twenty-seven of the sisters hadn't come back yet as they were biting people at a barbecue in next-door's garden. Fourteen had been squashed, twelve had discovered too late what it is that swallows swallow and one had got stuck to some sticky tape on a parcel and was on her way to Australia.

Young lady mosquitoes are horrible things. They bite anything they can get their nasty teeth into. They bite sleeping babies, happy budgerigars and even princesses. And when there's nothing else to bite they bite each other. Sid sat quietly in the corner and listened as the girls sat around telling amazing stories.

"I bit the postman three times," said one.

"That's nothing," said one called Sharon. "I flew right into a bathroom and bit an enormous lady with no clothes on seven times and I tripped over the soap and bruised three of my knees really badly."

"Well that's nothing at all," boasted a third sister. "I flew into an aeroplane, went all the way to America and back and bit twenty-three first-class passengers."

"You're all dead soft, you are," said the stupidest sister. "I'm so tough I jumped up and down inside the prickliest thistle in the whole world and bit myself twenty-seven million million times."

They went on for hours boasting away to each other, each sister trying to be braver and cleverer than the others. Sid listened wide-eyed to their stories. He was an honest little insect and didn't realize they were making them all up. Even when one said she had been to the moon in a spaceship, he believed her.

"And what have you been doing?" they asked Sid. As well as biting everything, young lady mosquitoes are very rude to everyone, have dreadful bad breath and lots of spots. Young boy mosquitoes on the other hand, because they only eat nectar and pollen, are kind and well behaved and have perfect skin.

"Have you been fighting a ferocious buttercup?" laughed the girls.

"Now just you leave young Sid alone," said his mother. "He's had more adventures today than any of you."

"Ooh, ooh," sneered the sisters, "did you get slapped by a daisy?"

"He got hit on the nose by some vicious fleas and doesn't want any trouble from you lot."

"Fleas, fleas. We hate fleas," shouted the girls and they all flew off to fight them, except Sharon who stayed behind to rub a dock leaf on her sore knees.

The next morning was perfect. A little cloud of soft mist hung above the pond as the sunshine crept over the trees. Birds stretched their wings and filled the air with a hundred new songs. The dragonflies flashed across the water while butterflies unfolded themselves and flew off across the nettles where busy ladybirds scuttled about. All down the little street the houses were quiet except for the clinking sound of milk bottles.

Sid sat on a twig breathing the damp sweet air. One by one his nasty sisters staggered out from under their leaves. They wandered about swearing a lot. They swore at the birds for being too noisy. They swore at the sunshine for being too bright. They swore at the butterflies for being too beautiful and they swore at the humans for still being in bed when they wanted to bite them. Most of all though, they swore at each other for being mosquitoes.

Eventually they all flew off and the pond was peaceful again. Sid flew deep inside an enormous waterlily. It was like being in a great big white tent. He shared his breakfast with a couple of wasps and a family of small brown beetles. One of the wasps was called Arnold and was about the same age as Sid.

Sid tried to tell Arnold about not being able to bite people but the wasp's ears were completely filled up with pollen and he couldn't hear him. Sid tried shouting.

"There's no need to shout," said Arnold.

"Sorry ."

"What did you say?" said Arnold.

"Nothing," muttered Sid and flew back to his twig. Nobody seemed to be interested in a little mosquito's problems. It wasn't that he didn't like pollen: it was very nice. And it wasn't that he wanted to be off with his sisters biting people all day long. All he wanted was one little bite, just to prove he could do it. That was all.

He decided to try again and set off towards the house next door. The curtains and windows were all open now. The people were cooking their breakfast and the cat was chasing birds round the edge of the lawn. As Sid sat on the kitchen window-sill, Arnold shot past and dived head first into a jar of marmalade.

Sid flew upstairs and into a bedroom. Inside, a small boy was getting dressed. As he leant over to try and do up his shoes, Sid landed on his neck and tried to bite him. He opened his mouth as wide as he could and pushed and shoved and clenched his fists. His ears began to ache and he went bright red in the face but all he could do was dribble.

The little boy went down to the kitchen and

Sid sat on the bedside table and cried.

At first there were so many tears in his eyes that he didn't notice the little man standing next to him. Then as his tears grew less he saw him. He had his back to Sid and didn't seem to have any clothes on. Sid tiptoed over and tried to bite him on the shoulder. To his amazement, his tiny teeth went right into the man and his mouth was filled with sugar.

Sid jumped for joy. Then he noticed the others. There was a whole crowd of them hiding in a box. They didn't seem to notice him at all so he went and bit every one of them. It was like sticking his head in the rose. He felt all happy and giddy. He had done it. He had actually bitten someone.

A bit later on the little boy came back and got the box of jelly babies, but by then Sid was back at the pond telling everyone about his adventure.

Billy Bear's Stumpy Tail

Retold by Nora Clarke

One wintry day, Billy Bear met Folly Fox slinking around a frozen pond. Folly Fox was trying to hide a net full of fish that he had just stolen.

"Where did you get such fine fish?" demanded Billy Bear.

"I caught them, of course," replied Folly quickly.

"I would really like to catch some fish," said Billy. "How did you do it?"

Now Folly Fox was jealous of Billy Bear's beautiful bushy tail, so he laughed and said, "It's easy, old friend. You slide on to the ice and cut a hole. Then you dangle your lovely bushy tail down, down into the water, sit on the ice and wait for the fish to nibble."

31

Billy Bear wrinkled his nose and pulled a long face.

"Isn't there another way to catch fish?" he growled.

"Not if you want such fine ones as these," said Folly Fox. "Anyway, it's easy. All you have to remember, dear friend, is to keep your tail in the hole. If you feel a few little nibbles or some pinches now and then, don't take any notice. Just remember that the fish are biting and hanging on to your long tail, and that the longer you wait the more fish you'll catch!"

Billy Bear growled and grunted suspiciously.

"How do I get the fish out of the water then?" he asked.

"That's easy for a strong bear," chuckled Folly. "First you give a great big push on to your right side then you push yourself over to your left side. Then you stand up quickly and start counting your fish."

Billy Bear was now convinced.

"My tail is much bigger than yours," he boasted, "so I'm sure to catch twice as many fish as you did."

He lumbered on to the ice, cut out a hole and sat down. Then he wiggled and waggled until his tail was dangling in the water. My, it was cold! But Billy thought about the wonderful dinner he would soon be having and pushed his tail down deeper into the hole.

Soon his tail was frozen fast in the pond and Billy was shivering with cold.

"Time to go," he chuckled in his growly voice. He rolled over on to his right side. Nothing moved. He pushed hard on to his left side. There was a little creak, creak. Then he

heaved himself up with all his strength, just as Folly Fox had told him to.

CRACK!

His tail snapped right off.

Sadly, Billy Bear crawled off the ice. He hadn't caught a single fish and he'd lost his beautiful tail. It never did grow again and that is why, to this day, all bears have stumpy tails.

The Fourth Life of Montezuma

Michael Morpurgo

As is well known, cats have nine lives. They can be used up quickly or, if the cat has a real instinct for survival, they can last for a long time. This particular cat, Montezuma, has already had three lucky escapes. The first when the farmer intended to drown all the kittens while they were very young. The second when Montezuma's mother deserted him. And the third when he fell into the duck pond from a high tree and nearly drowned. Now Montezuma faces his fourth life!

Montezuma spent the first summer and winter of his young life exploring his territory. During these months he awoke to his own potential as a hunter. The days were slept away peacefully by the kitchen stove; but at dusk, well fed and rested, he would slip out silently through the back door and be gone for the night.

Matthew saw little of him during this time. He might spot him skulking around the hedgerows on his way down the road to milking in the morning, or find him curled up in the barn when he went to fetch the hay. He loved to watch Montezuma basking in the summer sun, or chasing leaves in autumn, or stalking stealthily through the long grass in the orchard. But Matthew never played with him. For him, Montezuma was no plaything, just a companion that he liked to be with. He felt no proprietary rights over the cat. It was not his cat; he was Montezuma and that was enough.

Montezuma felt at ease in his home – most of the time. When Matthew and his mother were in the house he could sleep secure by his stove. For food he went to either of them, or both if he could get away with it, and always felt assured of a friendly response. He liked to sit on Matthew's knee and sharpen his claws on the shoulder of his jacket, rubbing up against his ear. But the sound of the father's footsteps was like an air-raid siren to him. If asleep he would awake, look frantically around and dash into the deepest, darkest corner he could find, and then flee the room as soon as he could. Matthew's father had never been deliberately cruel, not as such. But a cat knows when he is not welcome. Countless times Montezuma had been tipped out of his chair and chased out of the kitchen. It was true that Matthew's father had flung a boot in his direction once or twice when he had been yowling for his food, but he had never hit him. Now they simply avoided each other and had come to terms with that arrangement. They could live together if they lived apart.

Montezuma had grown into a huge, stripy ginger tom with a long tail that he carried proud and high, unless he was hunting. His ears were pointed sharply and were long enough to be those of a wild cat. The farmyard was his kingdom; he had made it so. There were other cats that occasionally strayed on to his land, but he made sure they didn't stay for long. Each intruder found to his cost that Montezuma stood his ground.

He was fast becoming a lethal hunter, with a preference for ambush. His favourite killing ground was in the hedgerows and ditches in the long barley field that ran along the lane down to the river. It was here he had served his hunting apprenticeship, discovered by trial and error the techniques that worked, and the habits of his prey. He knew every little track and hole; he learned to use the noise of the wind as camouflage and to lie in ambush as still as a log. He had come to gauge the speed of their reaction to his attack, to recognize and appreciate their individual capacity for retaliation and survival.

It was only with Sam, the farm's sheep and cattle dog, that Montezuma felt unsure of himself. Sam was never allowed in the house, so that the problem only arose outside the farmyard. Here, out in the open, they eyed each other at a distance and went their separate ways harbouring feelings of mutual suspicion and fear. Sam understood that this cat had come to stay by the frequency of their meetings and Montezuma knew that the dog belonged to the farm and was no direct threat to his feline supremacy of the farmyard.

Sam was a bushy black and white collie with long white teeth and a mouth that seemed to pant perpetually. He had that perception and intuitive intelligence that a good sheepdog should possess, and he sensed that it might be wise to give the young cat elbow room, for the moment anyway.

The two co-existed as only animals can with a degree of tolerance inspired by self-interest. But self-interest in two such close neighbours must inevitably clash, and so it did one Sunday afternoon on the front lawn outside the farmhouse.

As usual the bone from the Sunday joint of lamb had been handed to Sam, whose appetite for bones, or for anything else for that matter, was inexhaustible. Now Sam did not usually eat his bone at once – few bones were worth eating until they had lain in the earth for some weeks. His usual procedure was to trot down the lane to Mr Varley's vegetable garden, the softest bed of earth in the parish. There he would bury the bone busily, looking furtively over his shoulder all the while; and when he had nudged all the earth back over with his nose, he would return to the farm with an air of achievement, his nose caked a rich red-brown. For an intelligent dog this was a foolish thing to do. Everyone knew where he buried his bones, Mr Varley best of all, who dug up the bones whenever he discovered them and that was often enough. However, this particular afternoon Sam was tired, and it was hot, and the bone was big; so he lay down on the front lawn and gnawed contentedly in the sunshine.

Now Montezuma had always entertained hopes of the Sunday bone, and from his vantage point by the stove he watched Matthew leave the table and carry the great bone outside. He followed only on the off chance, and watched from the shrubbery as Matthew made the dog sit and take the bone gently in his mouth. The dog waited for Matthew to go back inside, standing possessively over his bone; and then he turned and padded on to the lawn, dropped his bone and lay down neatly, relishing the feast to come. Montezuma emerged cautiously from the shadows of the fuchsia, and sat down on the path a safe distance away. He had a tick in his ear and it needed scratching. The dog turned at the movement and growled a warning. He picked up his bone and moved away towards the garden wall.

This wall was a favourite place for Montezuma. It was flat on the top and could be used either for basking in the sun or as one of the best observation posts for local hunting. He had caught a wagtail from there only the week before. He retreated from the shrubbery and in a flanking movement ran round the other side of the wall and sprang up easily.

Sam was busily involved and unable at first to decide which end of the bone to begin. After much consideration he decided finally to stand up and strip it wherever the meat

42

was most plentiful. He planted one paw firmly on it and began his meal. From above him on the wall the cat watched, biding his time.

The phone rang back in the kitchen and Matthew's mother answered it as she always did. No one else ever moved when the phone rang. "Yes," she said, "Oh, we are sorry about that." And then, "I can't think how it can have happened. I'm so sorry." Matthew and his father stopped eating their apple pie and listened. "Through onto the garden. Oh deary me, deary me, it must be a terrible mess. Yes, yes. Well, we'll be right down. One of us'll be right down." She put the phone down and ran back into the kitchen. "It's your cows, Matthew; they're out in Mr Varley's garden, his vegetable garden. You'd best get down there. Hurry now."

"Take Sam," said his father. "And tell Mr Varley I'll be right down to help. Go on, lad, get going else there won't be any garden left." But Matthew was already gone, calling for Sam as he ran down the garden path.

Sam was reluctant to leave his bone. He had barely started his feast and he wouldn't leave his treasure out on the lawn exposed and vulnerable. "Come on, Sam. Leave it!" Matthew shouted at him and whistled him up. Sam compromised, picked up the bone and ran over towards him. "Not the bone, Sam, you blockhead. It's you I want. Drop it, drop it now." Sam obeyed, as he always did in the end, and dropped the bone in under the fuchsia hedge, out of sight. He backed out, cast an eye around to make sure that no one had seen him, and then sprinted away up the lane after Matthew, who was still whistling for him. Montezuma had watched it all from the top of his wall. He waited until boy and dog were out of sight and then he moved in, bounding across the lawn and into the fuchsia hedge. The bone was too heavy to move and anyway this was a perfect place to settle down. Montezuma crouched down on all fours and set to, still alert however to the possibility of surprise. His joy was unbounded as he found more and more layers of rich succulent red meat. He ate on, oblivious now to the world outside the shadows of the hedge. He had quite forgotten the dog and it never occurred to him that it might return to retrieve its bone.

Matthew and Sam were away for some time. It was not difficult to drive the cows back through the broken gate and out into the meadow again, but the explanations and condolences could not be hurried. Mr Varley had been a neighbour as long as Matthew had been alive and in all that time Matthew could not remember hearing a harsh word from him. And even now as the old man gazed out over his ruined vegetable garden, he simply shook his head sadly and puffed his pipe. He blamed no one. "S'pose it'll save me rotovating it," he said. "We've had a wonderful lot of vegetables this year, so I can't grumble."

Matthew tried to apologize and mentioned insurance money, but Mr Varley would have none of it. "Not your fault," he said. "Not anyone's fault. The cows broke through the gate. It's no use blaming them, is it now? And insurance you say. No, I'll not have any of that kind of thing. These things happen and there's nothing the insurance can do except pay me money; and it doesn't take money to dig over a vegetable patch, does it? You go home, my lad, and tell your Dad not to worry. We'll put it all to rights, you'll see."

Sam waited impatiently as the apologies dragged on. He had done his work and now he wanted to get back to his bone. When Matthew had finished apologizing for the umpteenth time he turned to go. Sam could wait no longer. At the bottom of the lane he left his master and ran on ahead, his mouth already watering in anticipation.

By the time Montezuma heard the dog, it was too late. He was caught unawares and was panicked into a hasty flight. He shot out of the back of the fuchsia hedge as the dog came in the front, but the dog had seen him on his bone and that was enough. The truce was broken and it was war.

Behind the fuchsia hedge was the piggery and the door was open as it always is in the summer to let the air in. Montezuma saw it as a way out. The pen doors at the back of the pig pens would be open and he could make his escape into the orchard and up a tree. But it was dark inside, darker than usual. He looked both ways but there was no time for a considered decision: the dog was close behind. Montezuma leapt the wall into the pen at the end of the piggery and landed in the muck at the other side. Then, and only then, did he realize that the pen doors were shut fast and that he was trapped. He whipped round and tried to leap the wall of the pen again. From there he might make it to the safety of the rafters. But the dog was already on the wall and looking down at him, his teeth gleaming white and his hackles up. The dog did not hesitate and Montezuma was hurled to the ground. He could feel the hot breath on his eyes and squirmed away from the teeth, rolling on to his back and slashing out at the face that bore down on him. He felt teeth sink into his leg, but took heart when he heard the dog yelp in pain as his claws flashed across the dog's nose drawing blood. Montezuma's ears were laid flat against his head, and he knew now that this was a fight to the death. Even if he could run, there was nowhere to run to. He had to fight it out. He set up a hideous yowling and spat viciously, swiping accurately at the dog's eyes as he came into the attack.

Sam was going for the throat. He had lost all traces of domesticity. He was back to the wolf. His teeth were bared, his face transformed from the soft, loving sheepdog to the ruthless killer. He had made two hits near the cat's throat conceding a scratched eye and nose, but his blood was up and no cat scratch could deter him now. He leapt forward again onto the cat and struck downwards, his teeth closing over the cat's ear. He had him now and shook him until he could hold the grip no longer.

Matthew heard the rumpus from half-way down the lane and he could guess what had happened. By the time he arrived there was no stopping Sam, who was quite beyond reason. He leant over the wall and tried to pull him off, but the dog turned on him like a cobra, snapping at his wrist. Matthew ran for the bucket of water he used for mixing the barley for the pigs. He filled it quickly from the tap and ran back, throwing it over Sam. Then he vaulted in over the rails, opened the pen doors to the outside and bundled Sam out whilst he was still shaking the water from his face.

Montezuma lay on his back, his front paws still instinctively sweeping the air above, blinded by the blood from his ear, Matthew talking to him, stroking his side to calm him. "All over, Monty," he said. "You're all right. You'll be all right." He picked him up carefully. "What did you do to get Sam all riled up like that? I've seen him kill a rat once, but he was never that angry. What did you do?"

Back in the kitchen they cleaned Montezuma up. The wounds were superficial, although his ear was badly torn and his leg would need stitching. Once the blood was cleared away, he looked more his old self. They took him to the vet who stitched him up and injected him; and for two or three days after he lay by his stove not eating and going out only when he had to. "He's sulking," said Matthew's mother.

"He's had his come-uppance," said Matthew's father. "That Sam taught him a thing or two."

"He's in pain," Matthew said. "You can tell, he must be in terrible pain."

But they all three had it wrong. Montezuma's pride had been hurt to the quick. He had made an elementary mistake in allowing himself to be taken by surprise. He felt no enmity towards the dog, but was consumed by a grim determination never to be caught off guard again.

The ear never straightened out after that, and his leg mended slowly. Within a week or so Montezuma was back on patrol, his pride damaged but intact. For his part, Sam had a gash across his face, a scratched eye and a torn nose; it was enough to persuade him to avoid another confrontation. The two eyed each other with mutual respect now, acknowledging each other as the king in his own world.

Olga's Day Off

Michael Bond

Guinea-pig Olga da Polga longs to see the world – a wish that is about to come true when she is bought by a little girl called Karen and leaves the pet shop for ever. In her new home with the "Sawdust" family (the name Olga gives them since an older, wiser guinea-pig told her that humans supply the sawdust that is necessary for guinea-pig comfort), Olga meets other pets – including Fangio, a hedge-hog. He tells her about life outside her run and encourages her to go adventuring.

In her heart of hearts Olga didn't really expect to go roaming for quite some time, if at all, so she was doubly surprised when the opportunity came the very next day. Like

51

most opportunities it happened unexpectedly, so that she had to make her decision at once before it passed her by.

In moving her run, someone – she wasn't sure who it was, for she was much too busy to notice – someone had been very careless and placed one corner of it on top of a small mound of grass. And this left a gap several inches high along part of one side.

Such a thing had never happened before and probably never would again. So Olga was left with no choice: it was now or never.

As soon as she felt she was alone she eased herself gently under the wooden frame, lowering her back and stretching herself out as far as she could, and suddenly she found herself on the other side.

She stood for a moment or two getting her breath back. All sorts of curious feelings were racing around inside her; part excitement, part fear, part elation at having done something so daring.

Even the air seemed different on the other side of her wire fence. Fresher somehow, and cleaner; full of the unknown.

Now she was ready for the big moment. The one she had been waiting for. The one she had dreamed about. She could start on her travels.

Which way should she go? Really, with the world at her feet and on every side as well it was hard to make a choice.

First of all she decided against the long, winding path leading back towards the house. There was no sense in risking capture quite so soon.

Then there was a vegetable patch near by, full of tempting cabbage leaves and lettuce plants, but she ruled this out too, for Mr Sawdust sometimes worked there and she might easily be spotted.

She wondered what Fangio the hedgehog would have done. Where was it he said he went to? The Elysian Fields? They couldn't be that far away. Not if he went there every evening.

Olga's mouth, which had been unusually dry until a moment ago, began to grow moist with anticipation at the thought of the good things to come.

"Wheeeeee!" she squeaked. "This is the life!" And without wasting any more time she bounded across the lawn in a series of short, sharp bursts until she found herself in the shrubbery.

The shrubbery!

Although she wouldn't have admitted it, even to herself, Olga found the shrubbery a trifle disappointing. From a distance it had always looked most inviting, with shady nooks and branches which waved gently in the breeze as if beckoning any passer-by to pause awhile and sample the delights within.

But far from it being full of delights Olga found it rather mucky, and very overgrown; chock-a-block with weeds and sharp brambles which parted easily enough but then immediately swung back again, cutting off her return with a dense barrier of thorns.

The further she went in the worse it became. Pushing, shoving, scrambling over dead twigs and branches, Olga forced her way deeper and deeper into the undergrowth.

It was all very well for Fangio. He had prickles to start off with. A few more were probably neither here nor there. But for a guinea-pig with only her fur to protect her – fur, moreover, which she'd always prided herself on keeping neat and clean – it was quite a different matter.

Halfway through the shrubbery Olga's fur already looked as if it had been dragged through a hedge backwards, and by the time the first few chinks of light appeared on the other side she hardly dared look down at herself for fear of what she might see.

At last, battered and bruised, scratched and ruffled, she burst through the remaining mass of tangled foliage and lay panting with exhaustion while she took stock of her new surroundings.

"Elysian Fields indeed!" she exclaimed bitterly.

As far as she could make out, Fangio's heaven on earth was nothing more than a rubbish dump, full of old tin cans and soggy bits of cardboard, and smelling strongly of bonfires.

As for food! Olga didn't really count two mangy-looking thistles and a bed of old nettles as being fit for a compost heap let alone a hungry guinea-pig.

As she contemplated it she grew gloomier and gloomier.

And at that moment, as if to add to her sorrows, it began to rain. First one spot, then another, then several more. Ping . . . ping . . . ping, ping, ping, they went on the old tin cans.

Then faster still and harder. Rat-tat-tat-tat-tat.

The spots became a downpour, the downpour a deluge. The burning embers of the bonfire sizzled out leaving behind an acrid smell. The nettles drooped beneath the weight. Trees added their drips to the cascade of water.

Olga made a dive for a near-by sheet of cardboard and sat shivering beneath it. Never, in all her life, had she felt so wet and miserable, so . . .

There was a rustle from somewhere near by and a moment later a familiar head poked out from beneath some leaves.

"Enjoying yourself?" asked Fangio. "Having fun?"

"*Enjoying* myself?" Olga stared at Fanigo. "Having *fun*?" she repeated. "I've never so unenjoyed myself in the whole of my life! If this is the Elysian Fields the sooner I'm back on my lawn the better! I've never seen anything so . . . so dismal!"

"Beauty," said Fangio, "is in the eye of the beholder. I must say that through *my* windows it looks lovely. Think of all the flies and insects there'll be when it stops raining."

Olga shuddered. Fangio was welcome to his insects. She hadn't the slightest wish to stay

57

ANIMAL STORIES FOR EIGHT YEAR OLDS

and see them. "If you ask me," she said, "*your* windows need cleaning. Good night!"

"Second on the right," called Fangio, as Olga stalked off, taking the long way home round the outside of the shrubbery. "Third on the left, then right again. Only mind you don't fall in the . . . oh!"

He broke off as an extra-loud splash sounded above the rain.

"You might have told me!" wailed Olga, as she clambered out of a mud-filled hole.

"You didn't give me a chance," said Fangio.

"Hedgehogs!" snorted Olga bitterly.

She had never felt so glad to see her run. Nor, for that matter, had she had such a welcome before. Judging by the whoops of delight that greeted her reappearance, it seemed as if everyone in the neighbourhood had been out looking for her.

"How nice to be back home," she thought. "How I could ever have wanted to leave I don't know."

"Where *have* you been?" cried Karen Sawdust, as she gathered Olga up in her arms. "We've been searching everywhere."

Mr Sawdust held up an umbrella for protection.

"Pooh!" said Mrs Sawdust. "She smells of bonfires."

Olga took a deep breath. "I've been to the Elysian Fields," she squeaked. "And I'm never, *ever* going there again!"

At least, that's what she meant to say, and if the squeaks themselves didn't exactly make sense to everyone around, the feeling that went into them made the meaning very clear indeed.

The Elephant's Child

Rudyard Kipling

In the High and Far-Off Times the Elephant, O Best Beloved, had no trunk. He had only a blackish, bulgy nose, as big as a boot, that he could wiggle about from side to side: but he couldn't pick up things with it. But there was one Elephant – a new Elephant – an Elephant's Child – who was full of 'satiable curiosity, and that means he asked ever so many questions. *And* he lived in Africa, and he filled all Africa with his 'satiable curiosities. He asked his tall aunt, the Ostrich, why her tail-feathers grew just so, and his tall aunt the Ostrich spanked him with her hard, hard claw. He asked his tall uncle, the Giraffe, what made his skin spotty, and his tall uncle, the Giraffe, spanked him with his hard, hard hoof. And still he was full of 'satiable curiosity! He asked his broad aunt the Hippopotamus, why her eyes were red, and his broad aunt, the Hippopotamus, spanked him with her broad, broad hoof; and he asked his hairy uncle, the Baboon, why melons tasted just so, and his hairy uncle, the Baboon, spanked him with his hairy, hairy paw. And *still* he was full of 'satiable curiosity! He asked questions about everything that he saw, or heard, or felt, or smelt, or touched, and all his uncles and his aunts spanked him. And still he was full of 'satiable curiosity!

One fine morning in the middle of the Precession of the Equinoxes this 'satiable Elephant's Child asked a new fine question that he had never asked before. He asked, "What does the Crocodile have for dinner?" Then everybody said, "Hush!" in a loud and dretful tone, and they spanked him immediately and directly, without stopping, for a long time.

By and by, when that was finished, he came upon Kolokolo Bird sitting in the middle of a wait-a-bit thorn-bush, and he said, "My father has spanked me, and my mother has spanked me: all my aunts and uncles have spanked me for my 'satiable curiosity; and *still* I want to know what the Crocodile has for dinner!"

The Kolokolo Bird said, with a mournful cry, "Go to the banks of the great grey-green, greasy Limpopo River, all set about with fever-trees, and find out."

That very next morning, when there was nothing left of the Equinoxes, because the Precession had preceded according to precedent, this 'satiable Elephant's Child took a hundred pounds of bananas (the little short red kind), and a hundred pounds of sugar-cane (the long purple kind), and seventeen melons (the greeny-crackly kind), and said to all his dear families, "Goodbye. I am going to the great grey-green, greasy Limpopo River, all set about with fever-trees, to find out what the Crocodile has for dinner." And they all spanked him once more for luck, though he asked them most politely to stop.

Then he went away, a little warm, but not at all astonished, eating melons, and throwing the rind about, because he could not pick it up.

He went from Graham's Town to Kimberley, and from Kimberley to Kharma's Country, and from Kharma's Country he went east by north, eating melons all the time, till at last he came to the banks of the great grey-green, greasy Limpopo River, all set about with fever-trees, precisely as Kolokolo Bird had said.

Now you must know and understand, O Best Beloved, that till that very week, and day, and hour, and minute, this 'satiable Elephant's Child had never seen a Crocodile, and did not know what one was like. It was all his 'satiable curiosity.

The first thing that he found was a Bi-Coloured-Python-Rock-Snake curled round a rock.

"'Scuse me," said the Elephant's Child most politely, "but have you seen such a thing as a Crocodile in these promiscuous parts?"

"*Have* I seen a Crocodile?" said the Bi-Coloured-Python-Rock-Snake, in a voice of dretful scorn. "What will you ask me next?"

"'Scuse me," said the Elephant's Child, "but could you kindly tell me what he has for dinner?"

Then the Bi-Coloured-Python-Rock-Snake uncoiled himself very quickly from the rock, and spanked the Elephant's Child with his scalesome, flailsome tail.

"That is odd," said the Elephant's Child, "because my father and my mother, and my uncle and my aunt, not to mention my other aunt, the Hippopotamus, and my other uncle, the Baboon, have all spanked me for my 'satiable curiosity – and I suppose this is the same thing."

So he said goodbye very politely to the Bi-Coloured-Python-Rock-Snake, and helped to coil him up on the rock again, and went on, a little warm, but not at all astonished, eating melons, and throwing the rind about, because he could not pick it up, till he trod on what he thought was a log of wood at the very edge of the great grey-green, greasy Limpopo River, all set about with fever-trees.

But it was really the Crocodile, O Best

Beloved, and the Crocodile winked one eye – like this!

"'Scuse me," said the Elephant's Child most politely, "but do you happen to have seen a Crocodile in these promiscuous parts?"

Then the Crocodile winked the other eye, and lifted half his tail out of the mud: and the Elephant's Child stepped back most politely, because he did not wish to be spanked again.

"Come hither, Little One," said the Crocodile. "Why do you ask such things?"

"'Scuse me," said the Elephant's Child most politely, "but my father has spanked me, my mother has spanked me, not to mention my tall aunt, the Ostrich, and my tall uncle, the Giraffe, who can kick ever so hard, as well as my broad aunt, the Hippopotamus, and my hairy uncle the Baboon, *and* including the Bi-Coloured-Python-Rock-Snake, with the scalesome, flailsome tail just up the bank, who spanks harder than any of them; and *so* if it's quite all the same to you, I don't want to be spanked any more."

"Come hither, Little One," said the Crocodile, "for I am the Crocodile," and he wept crocodile-tears to show it was quite true.

Then the Elephant's Child grew all breathless, and panted, and kneeled down on the bank and said, "You are the very person I have been looking for all these long days. Will you please tell me what you have for dinner?"

"Come hither, Little One," said the Crocodile, "and I'll whisper." Then the Elephant's Child put his head down close to the Crocodile's musky, tusky mouth, and the Crocodile caught him by his little nose, which up to that very week, day, hour and minute, had been no bigger than a boot, though much more useful.

"I think," said the Crocodile – and he said it between his teeth, like this – "I think today I will begin with Elephant's Child!"

At this, O Best Beloved, the Elephant's Child was much annoyed and he said, speaking through his nose, like this, "Led go! You are hurtig be!"

Then the Bi-Coloured-Python-Rock-Snake scuffled down from the bank and said, "My young friend, if you do not now, immediately and instantly, pull as hard as ever you can, it is my opinion that your acquaintance in the

large-pattern leather ulster" (and by this he meant the Crocodile) "will jerk you into yonder limpid stream before you can say Jack Robinson."

This is the way Bi-Coloured-Python-Rock-Snakes always talk.

Then the Elephant's Child sat back on his little haunches, and pulled, and pulled, and pulled, and his nose began to stretch. And the Crocodile floundered into the water, making it all creamy with great sweeps of his tail, and *he* pulled, and pulled, and pulled.

And the Elephant's Child's nose kept on stretching: and the Elephant's Child spread all his little four legs and pulled, and pulled, and pulled, and his nose kept on stretching: and the Crocodile threshed his tail like an oar, and *he* pulled, and pulled, and pulled, and at each pull the Elephant's Child's nose grew longer and longer – and it hurt him hijjus!

Then the Elephant's Child felt his legs slipping, and he said through his nose, which was now nearly five feet long. "This is too buch for be!"

Then the Bi-Coloured-Python-Rock-Snake came down from the bank, and knotted himself in double-clove-hitch round the Elephant's Child's hind-legs, and said, "Rash and inexperienced traveller, we will now seriously devote ourselves to a little high tension, because if we do not, it is my impression that yonder self-propelling man-of-war with the armour-plated upper deck," (and by this, O Best Beloved, he meant the Crocodile) "will permanently vitiate your future career".

That is the way all Bi-Coloured-Python-Rock-Snakes always talk.

So he pulled, and the Elephant's Child pulled, and the Crocodile pulled; but the Elephant's Child and the Bi-Coloured-Python-Rock-Snake pulled hardest; and at last the Crocodile let go of the Elephant's Child's nose with a plop that you could hear all up and down the Limpopo.

Then the Elephant's Child sat down most hard and sudden; but first he was careful to say "Thank You" to the Bi-Coloured-Python-Rock-Snake; and next he was kind to his poor pulled nose, and wrapped it all up in cool banana leaves, and hung it in the great grey-green, greasy Limpopo to cool.

"What are you doing that for?" said the Bi-Coloured-Python-Rock-Snake.

"'Scuse me," said the Elephant's Child, "but my nose is badly out of shape, and I am waiting for it to shrink."

"Then you will have to wait a long time," said the Bi-Coloured-Python-Rock-Snake. "Some people do not know what is good for them."

The Elephant's Child sat there for three days waiting for his nose to shrink. But it never grew any shorter, and, besides, it made him squint. For, O Best Beloved, you will see and understand that the Crocodile had pulled it out into a really truly trunk same as all Elephants have today.

At the end of the third day a fly came and stung him on the shoulder, and before he knew what he was doing he lifted up his trunk and hit that fly dead with the end of it.

"'Vantage number one!" said the Bi-Coloured-Python-Rock-Snake. "You couldn't have done that with a mere-smear nose. Try and eat a little now."

Before he thought what he was doing the Elephant's Child put out his trunk and plucked a large bundle of grass, dusted it clean against his fore-legs, and stuffed it into his own mouth.

"'Vantage number two!" said the Bi-Coloured-Python-Rock-Snake. "You couldn't have done that with a mere-smear nose. Don't you think the sun is very hot here?"

"It is," said the Elephant's Child, and

before he thought what he was doing he schlooped up a schloop of mud from the banks of the great grey-green, greasy Limpopo, and slapped it on his head, where it made a cool schloopy-sloshy mud-cap all trickly behind his ears.

"'Vantage number three!" said the Bi-Coloured-Python-Rock-Snake. "You couldn't have done that with a mere-smear nose. Now how do you feel about being spanked again?"

"'Scuse me," said the Elephant's Child, "but I should not like it at all."

"How would you like to spank somebody?" said the Bi-Coloured-Python-Rock-Snake.

"I should like it very much indeed," said the Elephant's Child.

"Well," said the Bi-Coloured-Python-Rock-Snake, "you will find that new nose of yours very useful to spank people with."

"Thank you," said the Elephant's Child. "I'll remember that; and now I think I'll go home to all my dear families and try."

So the Elephant's Child went home across Africa frisking and whisking his trunk. When he wanted fruit to eat he pulled fruit down from a tree, instead of waiting for it to fall as he used to do. When he wanted grass he plucked grass up from the ground, instead of going on his knees as he used to do. When the flies bit him he broke off the branches of a tree and used it as a fly-whisk: and he made himself a new, cool, slushy-squashy mud-cap whenever the sun was not. When he felt lonely walking through Africa he sang to himself down his trunk, and the noise was louder than several brass bands. He went specially out of his way to find a broad Hippopotamus (she was no relation of his), and he spanked her very hard, to make sure that the Bi-Coloured-Python-Rock-Snake had spoken the truth about his new trunk. The rest of the time he picked up the melon-rinds that he had dropped on his way to the Limpopo – for he was a Tidy Pachyderm.

One dark evening he came back to all his dear families, and he coiled up his trunk and said, "How do you do?" They were very glad to see him, and immediately said, "Come here and be spanked for your 'satiable curiosity."

"Pooh," said the Elephant's Child. "I don't

think you peoples know anything about spanking; but *I* do, and I'll show you."

Then he uncurled his trunk and knocked two of his dear brothers head over heels.

"O Bananas!" said they, "where did you learn that trick, and what have you done to your nose?"

"I got a new one from the Crocodile on the banks of the great grey-green, greasy Limpopo River," said the Elephant's Child. "I asked him what he had for dinner, and he gave me this to keep."

"It looks very ugly," said his hairy uncle, the Baboon.

"It does," said the Elephant's Child. "But it's very useful," and he picked up his hairy uncle, the Baboon, by one hairy leg, and hove him into a hornets' nest.

Then that bad Elephant's Child spanked all his dear families for a long time, till they were very warm and greatly astonished. He pulled out his tall Ostrich aunt's tail-feathers; and he caught his tall uncle, the Giraffe, by the hind-leg, and dragged him through a thorn-bush; and he shouted at his broad aunt, the

Hippopotamus, and blew bubbles into her ear when she was sleeping in the water after meals; but he never let any one touch Kolokolo Bird.

At last things grew so exciting that his dear families went off one by one in a hurry to the banks of the great grey-green, greasy Limpopo River, all set about with fever-trees, to borrow new noses from the Crocodile. When they came back nobody spanked anybody any more; and ever since that day, O Best Beloved, all the Elephants you will ever see, besides all those you won't, have trunks precisely like the trunk of the 'satiable Elephant's Child.

Yucky Ducky

David Henry Wilson

Once upon a time there was a Mother Duck who laid six eggs. Five of the eggs were extremely beautiful, and the sixth was extremely ugly.

"Look at our five extremely beautiful eggs!" cried Mother Duck.

"Look at your sixth extremely ugly egg!" cried Father Duck. "Let's throw it in the river."

But Mother Duck had once heard a story about an ugly duckling that had turned into a beautiful swan, and so she would not let her husband throw the sixth egg away. Instead she sat on it, together with the other eggs, week after week, as patiently as a picture of a statue of a stuffed duck in a glass case.

Occasionally she would take a look at the eggs, and if anything five of them looked even more beautiful, and the sixth looked even more ugly. And then at last the eggshells began to break. One, two, three, four, five shells went pop, crackle, quack, and out came five extremely beautiful ducklings. And then the sixth egg went pop, crackle, ouch! Oh! Ah! And out came ... ugh! ... what a sight! It was presumably a duckling, but a more horrible, hideous, yuck of a duck it was impossible to imagine.

At first sight of him, Father Duck announced that he was going fishing, and was never seen again. As for the five extremely beautiful ducklings, they waddled round their ugly brother, beaking him with their bills and bumping him with their bottoms, quacking "Yucky Ducky!" and making him cry. It wasn't, of course, a normal weepy wahwoo cry, but a harsh and air-splitting quaaaaaaark, which made even the local earwigs cover their ears with their wigs.

"Never mind, Yucky," said Mother Duck. "One day you'll turn into a beautiful swan, and make Mummy very proud of you."

Then she took them all out on the river. The five beautiful ducklings swam smoothly and gracefully behind her, while the ugly duckling made all kinds of clumsy splashy movements and finally sank to the bottom of the river with a cry of "He-e-e-lplug glug glug!" Fortunately, Mother Duck saw him sink. Quickly and quackly she dived to the bottom and pulled him up to the surface. He was covered with mud and hardly breathing. Mother Duck laid him on the river bank and gave him the quack of life, whereupon he opened his amazingly ugly, look-in-all-directions eyes and began to quaaaaaaark.

"Quaaaaaaark!" he cried "Quaaaaaaark, I can't even ... quaaaaaark ... swim!"

"Mucky Yucky can't even swim!" jeered his extremely beautiful brothers and sisters.

"Never mind, darling," said Mother Duck. "One day you'll turn into a beautiful swan and swim better than all of us."

Then she took her ducklings for a waddle through the woods. The five beautiful ducklings waddled steadily and proudly behind their mother, while the ugly duckling kept falling over or bumping into trees. Finally he got caught in a gorse bush and couldn't get free.

"He-e-e-lp ouch . . . oaf . . . ark . . . quaaa-aaaark!" he cried.

"Yucky's stucky!" jeered his brothers and sisters.

Mother Duck pecked the thorny branches away from the unlucky stucky Yucky, and he managed to stagger clear before he tripped over the root of a tree, stumbled, tumbled, and banged his beak on the bark.

"Quaaaaaaark!" he cried. "I can't even . . . quaaaaaaark . . . waddle!"

"Never mind, lovey," said Mother Duck. "One day you'll turn into a beautiful swan and waddle better than all of us."

Then she took them for a toddle along a country road where there were no gorse bushes, no muddy water, no holes to fall down, no roots to trip over, and no trees to bump into. All there was, as it turned out, was a large lorry which had chosen exactly the same route as Mother Duck. And in less time than it takes to say "Quack!" or "Quaaaaaaark!" or "I say, isn't that a rather large lorry coming towards us?" the lorry had run over one mother duck and five extremely beautiful ducklings who suddenly became five extremely flattened ducklings. And Yucky, who had tripped over his own feet and fallen at the side of the road, now found himself all alone in the world. At this moment some might have called him "Lucky Yucky", but he sat at the side of the road and quaaaaaaarked as loudly as if he had been run over himself. Even louder, in fact, since a run-over duckling probably wouldn't quaaaaaaark at all.

The lorry driver climbed out of his lorry, and when he saw the line of duck and ducklings all squashed in the road, he was a very sorry lorry driver. But there was nothing he could do. Then he heard Yucky quaaaaaaarking and went to have a look. One look was all he needed.

"Goodness gracious me!" he said (or words to that effect). "Wot a 'orrible sight. You're an even worse mess than yer brothers an' sisters!"

There was clearly nothing he could do for Yucky either, and so he climbed into his lorry and drove away.

"Quaaaaaaark!" cried Yucky "I can't even . . . quaaaaaaark . . . get myself run over!"

He waited for a voice to tell him that one day he would turn into a beautiful swan and get himself run over better than all of them, but no voice spoke. And so he sat at the side of the road feeling very unrun-over, ugly and alone.

Now, although Yucky was extremely ugly he was not extremely stupid. Stupid, yes, but not *extremely* stupid. And he finally came up with what was really rather a clever thought. If he was one day going to turn into a beautiful swan, maybe he could find some swans now and ask them to look after him. He didn't actually know what swans looked like, or where they lived, but he did know that a live swan was more likely to help him than a dead duck.

The only clue Yucky had was the fact that swans were beautiful, and so as he waddle-totter-trip-fell along the road, he looked out for something beautiful. While he was looking, he happened to trip-fall into a ditch and, as he lay sprawled in the water, he found one of his eyes gazing at a very beautiful creature that was resting on a wild flower beside the ditch. It had red and gold wings with black spots, and although it was a lot smaller than himself, he thought it would be nice to be so beautiful.

"Excuse me," he said, "but are you a swan?"

"No, my deah," said the creature. "Ai'm a

buttahflay. And whay do you think Ai maight be a swan?"

"Because you're so beautiful," said Yucky, "and I know swans are beautiful."

"Ai am beautiful, that's twue," said the butterfly, "but swans are gweat big things, whaile Ai'm extwemely delicate and fwagile. No, you poor ugly cweature: a buttahflay, thet's what Ai am."

And so now Yucky knew that swans were great big things, and he waddle-toddled away into the forest to search for them.

Before long he saw a great big thing that was very beautiful indeed. It was standing beneath a tree and it had four legs, large eyes, and huge antlers on its head.

"Excuse me," said Yucky, "but are you a swan?"

"A swan?" bellowed the animal. "Me? Mighty, massive, majestic me? No, you poor ugly little whatever-you-are, I'm a stag. King of the forest – though don't tell the lion I said so."

"I know that swans are big and beautiful," said Yucky, "and you're big and beautiful, so I thought you were a swan."

"Swans," said the stag, "may seem big and beautiful to you, but nothing, absolutely nothing, could be as big or as beautiful as I am. Besides, swans are birds. Whoever heard of a bird that could be compared with a stag? Whoever heard of *anything* that could be compared with a stag?"

And so now Yucky knew that swans were beautiful great big birds, and he stagger-stumbled further into the forest to see if he could find them.

Before long he saw a great big bird that was very beautiful indeed. It was perched on the branch of a tree, and it had huge wings, glittering eyes, and a curved beak.

"Excuse me," said Yucky, "but are you a swan?"

"You gotta be kiddin'," said the bird. "A swan? Me? Do I look like a swan?"

"Well," said Yucky, "I was told swans are great big beautiful birds, and you're big and beautiful . . ."

"Ain't it de truth!" said the bird. "I'm de biggest an' beautifullest boid in de forest, an' I could eat a swan for breakfast. I'd eat you, too, if you wasn't so unappetizin'. Eagle, dat's me. King o' de boids."

"Quaaaaaaark!" cried Yucky. "I shall never . . . quaaaaaaark . . . find the swans!"

"Aw quit quarkin'," snapped the eagle. "It gets on my noives. Go an' jump in de river – dat's where de swans hang out."

And so Yucky totter-tumbled away in search of the river. But he was now very tired. If he had been bumping into things and falling over before, he was now bumping-bumping and falling-falling twice as much. At last his right foot tripped over his left foot and he fell down beside a muddy pond. He didn't bother to get up

"Quaaaaaaark!" he cried.

"Aaaaaaark!" cried a voice next to his right ear. "Quaaaaaaark!" said Yucky again, thinking it had been an echo.

"Aaaaaaark!" said the echo.

Yucky looked up and saw the ugliest creature he had ever seen (not counting Yucky himself, though he had not actually seen himself, since mirrors don't grow on trees). The creature was brown and squat, had long hind legs with webbed feet, short front legs, big eyes, and a wide mouth, and it was covered with warts.

"Crikey!" exclaimed Yucky. "Aren't you ugly!"

"Croakey!" exclaimed the creature (which was a toad). "I'm not as ugly as you!"

"You're uglier than me!" cried Yucky.

"Nothing could be uglier than you!" cried the toad.

"When I grow up," said Yucky, "I shall be a beautiful swan."

"When I grow up," said the toad, "I shall be a handsome prince."

"Why don't you both grow up," said a passing rat, "and be yourselves."

"Don't take any notice of him," said the toad. "He's just a dirty rat."

Then the toad told Yucky that he was searching for a palace, where he would live happily ever after. Yucky said that if he ever bumped into a palace he would let the toad know. Then Yucky told the toad that he was searching for a river, where all his troubles would be over.

"You're lucky," said the toad. "Rivers are easy to find."

"Nothing's easy for me to find," said Yucky. "Sometimes I can't even find my own feet."

Yucky and the toad became good friends, and they decided to stay together until they became a swan and a prince. They waited a long time. The only change that Yucky saw in the toad was that he seemed to get smaller and uglier. The toad, on the other hand, thought Yucky was growing bigger and uglier. And Yucky himself certainly felt that he was bigger. He also found out that he could not only swim a few yards in the pond but even fly a few yards through the air – before crashing in a crumpled heap on the earth. All this seemed to be a sign that he had now grown up, and if he had grown up, then he must surely have turned into a swan.

"Well," he said to the toad, "that's it."

"That's what?" asked the toad.

"I'm a swan," said Yucky.

"You're kidding," said the toad.

"No, I'm not," said Yucky. "I'm swanning."

"If you're a swan," said the toad, "then I'm a handsome prince."

"Quackle quackle quackle!" cackled Yucky. "I've never seen a handsome prince as ugly as you!"

"Uckle uckle uckle!" chuckled the toad. "You're so ugly, you're more like a swine than a swan!"

"Well, you're not a handsome prince," said Yucky.

"I know," said the toad. "And you're not a swan."

But although the toad knew he was not a handsome prince, Yucky was still sure he was a swan, and so he decided to set out for the river to find his fellow swans. It so happened that the toad had found out where the river was.

"All you have to do," he said, "is follow the track straight over that hill. That is, if you *can* ever go straight over anything."

"What are *you* going to do?" asked Yucky.

"I'm going to look for the road to the palace," said the toad.

And so the two of them said goodbye to each other and went their separate ways.

"Hope you find the right roadie, Toadie!" called Yucky.

"Stay on the trackie, Quackie!" shouted the toad.

Yucky waddled (and fell) and flew (and fell) along the track which led over the hill and finally down to the river. It was a clear, calm, sunny day and, as he stood on the river bank where he had spent so many miserable days in the past, he felt that he had come home. And when, out in the middle of the river, he caught sight of two graceful, long-necked, elegant white birds gliding through the water, he just knew that these were swans and he was one of them.

"Hullo, there!" he cried, and dived with a great sploshy splash into the water.

The swans took no notice, but Yucky waggled his feet and flapped his wings and managed to crash-whoosh his way towards them.

"Hullo, there!" he cried again. "Wait for me!"

"Are you speaking to us?" asked the male swan.

"Yes!" puffed Yucky. "You're swans, aren't you?"

"Of course we're swans," said the female swan.

"Great!" said Yucky. "Then we can all be swans together."

"We don't want riff-raff like that around here," said the female swan. "Marcel, chase him off."

Marcel, the male swan, immediately raced towards Yucky and gave him a fearful peck on the bottom.

"Quouch!" cried Yucky.

"Quack off!" cried Marcel.

"But I'm not an ugly duckling any more!" howled Yucky. "I'm a swan like you!"

"Don't be insulting!" said Marcel, and added a second peck to the first.

Yucky didn't wait for a third peck. Quaaaaaaarking with pain and fear, he whoosh-crashed his way back towards the river bank, while Marcel and his wife sailed serenely away down the river, discussing the lowered tone of the neighbourhood.

Yucky stood on the river bank and sadly

watched them go. Why hadn't they welcomed him? Why had they called him riff-raff? Why had they pecked his bottom?

Yucky's head dropped with the weight of his disappointment, and he found himself gazing down into the calm water. And the reflection that he saw there gave him the answer to all his questions. He had been right: he had grown up. And now, instead of being an extremely ugly duckling, he had turned into an extremely ugly duck.

Chut the Kangaroo

Dorothy Cottrell

When the three men had finished skinning their game – two kangaroos – they took a last look around. Suddenly one of them saw the infant "joey" whose mother had been killed the night before.

"**J**ove!" said the man. "There's a little fellow!"

He pounced upon Chut, who simply shrank into himself and waited for the last spasm of the terror which was death.

"He's a little beauty," said the man. "I'm going to take him home to my wife." He held Chut up ridiculously by the scruff of the neck and poked him with his finger. Then the man looked puzzled. "He's all scratched and he's been cut across the back – looks like an eagle's had him . . . Say, I guess he must have belonged to the doe that got away last night! Poor little nipper!"

"Let's take him and give him a drink!" the other men suggested. Gathering up the skins, they moved off round the head of the dam, Chut hanging limp and hopeless under the big man's arm.

At the camp, back over the ridge, there was discussion as to how the baby should be fed and some facetious suggestions of sending for Dr Holt's Book on Infant Feeding. Then the first man said: "He won't drink unless he's upside down . . ." So they got an old pair of trousers and tied a knot in one leg at the knee, and hung the trousers to a tree limb by the back strap. Then they held Chut up before it. He looked at it in confusion.

"Better let him get in himself," said the big man. He gave Chut a friendly pinch. It worked. Instinctively Chut grasped the edge of the trousers, lowered his head, and bracing his hoppers against the big man's stomach, turned his dexterous somersault into the warm depths of the leg! Once again he was swinging as a kangaroo should swing. He was enclosed; safe. He gave a feeble, twittering chitter.

One of the other men stepped forward and presented him with the end of a bit of insulating rubber, from which the wire had been withdrawn, and whose other end was in a tin of milk.

Chut sucked, sucked again. Milk was in his mouth. He gave little ticking sounds of bliss, and, still drinking, he fell asleep in the maternal embrace of the trouser leg.

Chut's wound healed. The men were good to him. He learned the new smells of fire-smoke, and potatoes roasting in ashes; the mellow smell of coffee and the sharp tang of tea, the odours of frizzling bacon and grilling chops; of tobacco smoke by a camp fire under stars; and the sneeziness of raw flour, and the smell of men. He learned that fire was hot and kerosene nasty. His ears attuned themselves to new sounds, for the men were as noisy as the wilderness was silent. Clatter of plates, loud jests and louder laughter, galloping of horses and clanging music of horse-bells, ceased to appal him.

When, after a month's work on the lower run, the big man returned home, Chut went with him, swinging securely in one leg of a pair of old trousers attached to the man's saddle. Arrived at the small, tree-set homestead, the man was met by his young wife; and Chut, observing the meeting through a cigarette hole in the trouser leg, sensed that it was affectionate.

"I've brought you home a baby!" the big man said, untying the old trousers from the pommel of the saddle, and handing them to her – one of the legs showing plumply bulged. She took the garment hesitatingly, peering into the top, perceived Chut where he waited in bright-eyed, velvet-furred minuteness, and exclaimed: "Oh, the darling, sweet, tiny thing!"

The man dismounted, and stepped up to her.

"He is so little!" she said. "And so soft and fat."

At that the man took her in his arms.

"What," she said, "will we call him?"

But, squeezed between the big man and his

wife, Chut was very uncomfortable. He gave a surprisingly loud and indignant cry of protest. "Chut! Chut! Chut-ch-ch-ch-ch!"

So he was called "Chut", which prior to this time had simply been his staple of conversation and announcement of his presence.

During the day he followed the girl about like a little dog. At night he slept in the trousers which swung by the big outside fireplace – these habiliments coming to be known as "Chut's pants".

He would come when the woman called him, and somersault neatly into her lap as she sat on the steps. There, lying on his back, he took his supper to the accompaniment of small kicks of pleasure.

He was also promoted to all the dignity of a real baby's bottle instead of the bit of insulating tube fastened to a condensed milk tin with which the men had nourished him in camp. The dogs were introduced to him one by one, it being forcefully explained to them that he was taboo.

There was soft green grass in which he might roll, and many trailing pepper trees beneath which to play small solitary games. In short, his world was eminently satisfactory – save for one thing.

There was at the homestead a ridiculously fat, excessively bumptious lamb, by name William Mutton. To William had belonged the baby's bottle before Chut took it over, and William harboured a dark and bitter resentment at the loss of his bottle. He was an incredibly greedy lamb. And, although fed to repletion, he was forever sucking at the woman's fingers, at her apron strings, at the tassels of blinds – anything. A moment after having eaten until he could eat no more, he called pitifully of his semi-starvation. To see anyone else eat appeared to cause him pain.

"That lamb," said the big man, "is not, I fear, of a generous turn of mind. He might even be described as a little grasping."

At least, to see Chut being nourished appeared to sear the very soul of William Mutton. Chut had been eager to be friendly. Upon one of the first occasions when he had ventured on a little walk by himself, he had come upon the lamb around a trailing pepper branch. The baleful gleam in William Mutton's eye meant nothing to him. All he saw was a creature of approximately his own size who might possibly want to sport a little.

Chut drew himself up to his now twenty-five-inch height, and standing poised upon the arch of his lower tail and the tips of his toes he gave a few stiff, bouncing little sidehops – the kangaroo's invitation to play.

"Chut!" he remarked affably. "Chut! Ch-ch!"

William's head dropped lower. He focused evilly upon the cream-velvet rotundity of Chut's stomach. Then, with a malevolent "Baa", he charged upon the little kangaroo.

His round woolly head met Chut's silk-furred stomach with a resonant plop. Chut grunted and fell, kicking, while William strolled triumphantly about his business without even deigning to look back.

After that he took especial pains to make the little kangaroo's life wretched. He specialized in knocking Chut down from different directions and in varying localities. He learned his victim's weaknesses and played upon them . . . .

Persistent persecution will, of course, develop wariness in the most confiding creature, and as Chut grew older he became harder to catch. On the other hand, if William's butts became less frequent, they became harder: for William was a particularly hefty young sheep and in addition he was growing horns – only nubby buds as yet, but distinctly uncomfortable when applied to Chut's person.

Then, about the time that, greatly to his own surprise, Chut outgrew his trouser leg, the big man, whose name Chut now knew was Tom Henton, brought in two little does who were just a shade smaller than Chut had been at the time of his capture.

And the woman whom everyone but Tom Henton called Mrs Henton christened them Zodie and Blue Baby, and Chut promptly adopted them both. He would sit for twenty minutes at a time chitting and whispering into the mouths of their sleeping bags. He nosed them, and pulled in a manly, masterful way at their ears.

When they were old enough to come out to

play, he romped with them, and at times put his little arms round both their necks so that the three small heads were drawn close together. Then he led them upon little gallops beneath the trees.

Of the two little does, Blue Baby was his darling. For as gentlemen allegedly prefer blondes, so male kangaroos seem melted by a blue tone in a lady's fur: experienced old kangaroo hunters having often noticed that amongst all the mouse-hued harem an "old man" will make a pet of a blue doe.

And Blue Baby was furred in an exquisite shade of smoke blue, brighter than the bluest of squirrel fur, and her stomach and chest were clear, cream-velvet. Her slender little tail, hoppers and hands, were dark, her eyes dark and dewy-soft. But for some reason she was slightly lame.

She could travel all right on her hoppers and hands, but when she attempted to hop in an upright position she stumbled and fell. Hence she was always left behind in the races. And Chut would always circle back for her, and pass and repass her – as though he did not want her to be left out.

When she too outgrew the trousers, he slept with one little arm about her neck, their attitudes touchingly like those of sleeping children.

As an evil shadow on the sunshine of young romance hovered the malevolent-eyed Mutton, always ready to charge upon the unguarded Chut and knock the wind out of him.

But Chut was growing miraculously fast now. His chubbiness had gone from him, likewise the legginess of youth that followed it. He was nowhere near his full growth – would not reach it for a long time yet – but he was strong-boned, erect, with the muscles swelling deeply beneath the skin of his forearms and back. When he drew himself up, he was almost as tall as Mrs Henton. But at her call his great body still somersaulted innocently into her lap, and, when he could inveigle her into giving it to him, he still adored his bottle. He still lay on his back in the sun and played with his toes, and he still had an infantile attachment for the pair of trousers which had been his foster-mother.

After the manner of kangaroos he was consumingly curious. He wanted to see everything. He tasted everything, and loved bread and sugar.

Gentle and awkward on the slippery oilcloth, the three kangaroos would come begging about the dinner table for pieces of sugared bread, which they had been taught to carry outside before eating – although they often fell to temptation and snatched little bites as they went.

One day they had just got their precious sweetened bread and carried it out beneath the big pepper tree, when the marauding Mutton bore down upon them.

Chut and Zodie hopped out of the way, still holding their crusts, but Blue Baby was clumsy and in her agitation she dropped her bread.

Had William Mutton contented himself with merely taking the bread, it is doubtful if Chut would have noticed, but William, who in the past had always confined his attacks to Chut, suddenly decided that Blue Baby would do as well. And, with an evil "Baa", he charged her – sending her sprawling to the grass, chittering little exclamations of fright!

Chut looked up. Blue Baby chittered more alarmedly.

Chut dropped his bread and drew himself up on to toes and lower tail-arch, and made a few little bouncing dancing steps: a kangaroo's invitation to play or fight.

William Mutton had seized Blue Baby's bit of bread. Blue Baby still lay on her back in the grass, too astonished and frightened to rise.

Chut danced up to the sheep, his arms hanging out from his sides like a belligerent man's, his ribs expanded.

"Chut!" he cried harshly. "Chut! Chut! Chut!"

"Baa!" said William Mutton, contemptuously masticating. Next moment he was grabbed by the backwool, and one of Chut's long hind toes kicked him dexterously in the side, tearing out a hunk of wool as it ripped downward.

Like most bullies, William was an arrant coward. He bleated and leapt for safety. Chut clawed for his fat rump as he went, and pulled out more wool. William gathered pulsing momentum of baa-punctuated bounds. And Chut followed him, trying vainly for another kick – for anything as low as a sheep is a most awkward thing for a kangaroo to fight.

William fled wildly, crying for undeserved help. The swimming pool lay before them. At its edge William, who dreaded water, tried to wheel, and at the same moment gave a foolish, prancing rear-up!

This was fatal. A kangaroo cannot kick

well unless it can embrace the thing it is kicking. William's semi-leap brought him to the perfect height for Chut's best attentions. Chut's hands clutched the miserable sheep's neck, his strong-muscled arms tightened like virgin rubber as he clasped the writhing form of Mutton to his chest. With "chuts" and nickers of rage he delivered a whirlwind of kicks to his victim's stomach.

They were his first fighting kicks, and poorly directed – which was as well for William – but they drew bleats and wool at each application.

Then Chut lost his balance, released his hold for a moment, and William Mutton made a frantic leap for safety – into the pool!

Tom Henton, who had been an amused and astonished spectator of the fight, fished him out again. He emerged a sadder and wiser sheep, to whom a kangaroo's stomach was forever after invisible.

But Chut had tasted the hot wine of his own strength. He wanted someone to wrestle with! During the next days he hopped pompously about the garden enclosure, with his arms swinging a little out from his sides, his chest expanded and his spine curving backward with his erectness. He stood in front of Tom Henton as he came in of an evening, and made little sparring sideward hops on the extreme tips of his toes and ridged arch of his lower-tail.

One night the man laughed, saying: "All right then!" and put on boxing gloves to spar with the great young kangaroo. Mrs Henton had viewed the proceeding with alarm, for a kangaroo can disembowel a man or dog with a single scythe-rip of his hooked foot. But it was soon obvious that Chut fully understood the playful nature of the battle. He would no more have thought of letting his strength go than the man would have dreamed of putting his full weight behind a blow to Chut's jaw.

They clinched and swayed, they sparred and side-stepped, until Tom leapt back to wipe the sweat from his streaming face, and Chut panted, and cooled his arms by licking them to the semblance of dark rubber.

After this they wrestled almost every evening, and so "boxing" was added to Chut's tricks. At the end of a match, if he had "played" well, he got his little bit of bread and sugar – which he held in both hands and smeared disgustingly about his face.

It happened that the summer had been a very busy one for Tom Henton, and so he had engaged a "yardman" to look after the cows, and the wood-chopping, and the home vegetable garden. The youth who performed these duties was not prepossessing, his manner alternating between over-familiarity and sullenness, while his progress was exasperatingly deliberate. A seemingly permanent cigarette drooped from his lower lip, and he did not remove it as he spoke.

Still, labour was hard to get, and Tom Henton decided to keep the man until after the shearing.

William Mutton, who had no decent pride, would follow the yardman about in the hope of sneaking something from the fowls' bucket, but Chut ignored the youth's existence.

At least he ignored it until the shearing-time came.

The shearing shed and the sheep yards

were some half-mile from the house, but dust clouds stirred up from the drafting pens had come to Chut's nostrils with exciting scents of heat and sheep trailing from them. He caught far, murmurous bleatings, stockwhip cracks, distant shoutings . . .

And Chut wanted to go and see the shearing! He plainly indicated as much as Tom Henton was riding out of a morning: placing one horny, confiding hand upon the man's stirrup in hint that he was coming too. When, in spite of this, he was left behind, he hopped up and down inside the enclosure fence, thumping his twenty-pound tail deliberately and loudly upon the ground as an intimation of his extreme displeasure and agitation.

Tom Henton had given very definite instructions that the big kangaroo was not to be let out during shearing. He didn't want any tricks played upon Chut, and shearer-men have an odd sense of humour. Also there was always the chance of a sudden fright temporarily stampeding the kangaroo into the bush, and there he might be shot in mistake for a wild 'roo.

"Keep the gates shut," said Tom to the yardman. "And be dead sure they're fastened!" The youth spat and said "OK," but he had already resolved to take Chut down to the shed and stage a demonstration fight for a shilling-a-man admission.

To do this he waited until a Sunday afternoon, when Tom Henton was away bringing in sheep for Monday's "run", and Mrs Henton was lying down asleep.

Chut was also dozing under a pepper tree, with his legs sticking absurdly skyward, when the yardman whispered his name and enticed him with bread. But he took no notice until he saw the man open the gate. Then he followed, and continued following all the way to the shed: hopping behind the yardman's pony. At the shed he was embarrassed by the number of people and by the great wool-smelling iron rooms.

And, because the yardman was at least familiar, Chut followed him more closely still.

The yardman collected his shillings, and then led the big puzzled kangaroo into the wool room, while the audience seated itself upon the stacked bales of wool.

The yardman fastened on Chut's gloves and put on gloves himself: then he stepped out in a fighting attitude, saying: "Come on, Boy!"

Chut didn't want to come on, however. He was rather frightened by the laughter, the voices, and the smoke haze. Also he was particular about the people with whom he fought. His boxing was a love-game he played with Tom Henton.

"Put 'em up!" said the yardman, tapping Chut lightly upon the cheek. Chut sat far back on his haunches and chutted offendedly: a small sound in appealing contrast to his size. The man danced up and down before him and poked him in the ribs. Chut protested with dignity, but made no attempt to fight.

Grumbling began amongst the members of the audience.

"Hey, where's my shilling?" "Aw, I'm going home." "This is a dead show!" "*That* the best he can do?"

The yardman began to lose his temper. The fool beast fought quick enough when he wanted to! He was going to fight now! He hit

Chut rather ungently in the lower ribs. Chut grunted and looked about with great soft eyes – appealing for fair play! He was not hurting this man, and the man was getting rough with him!

Still he obviously had no intention of sparring. He was a picture of gentle, slightly pompous, and much-offended courtesy. He looked about for Tom or Mrs Henton . . .

"Garn! He's no fighter!" yelled the men. "Where's them shillin's?"

The yardman was hot, nervous and exasperated. His audience was threatening to walk out on him. Unnoticed by any of the spectators, he snatched the live cigarette from his lips, and holding it hidden in his glove he pressed the glowing tip upon Chut's sensitive nose. Pressed it hard, twisted it.

The sequel happened so quickly that no one was sure of just how Chut got the silly gloves off. But the next second he was holding the screaming yardman in his powerful hug, and, having torn the youth's trousers off, was operating on his shirt-tail to the accompaniment of a ripping, rag-bag sort of sound!

As the shirt vanished, Chut's great-toe plied artistically for a hold upon the yardman's abdomen. With his forehand he clawed the yardman's hair. His eyes had a new, murderous light. He shook and bent the man in his embrace! . . . .

Then half the men in the shed were on him. Beating at him with rails, prodding him with wool-hooks.

He dropped the frantic and badly clawed yardman, and wheeled – to receive a bewildering rain of blows!

His swift anger was already over. All he wanted was to go home. He burst through the threatening circle and hopped majestically out of the wool-room door, gathering momentum as he went, and moving homeward, not with the frantic thirty-feet-at-a-bound of a frightened doe, but rhythmically covering a steady fifteen feet at a hop. One man fired after him, but the shots went wide.

It was at this stage that Tom Henton rode up to the shed, to be horrified at the tale of Chut's ferocity and the spectacle of the bleeding man. With relief he found that no vital injury had been done, but it was with a heavy heart that he at last rode home. The shearers, none of whom had observed the cigarette outrage, had assured him that the yardman had simply been inviting Chut to a friendly sparring bout!

If Chut was going to make unprovoked attacks like that, he was not safe . . .

Mrs Henton was likewise shocked at the account of the yardman's injuries. But she refused to believe that Chut's anger had been unprovoked.

"We simply couldn't shoot him!" she cried. "Why, if he could tell us what happened he could very likely explain everything! Oh Tom, he is so dear and funny!"

"We can't get his side of it," said the man. "And the fact remains that if he hadn't been beaten off he might have killed someone."

"You *can't* shoot him!"

"I can't see how we can keep him. I'd be afraid for you, honey. Afraid to have him loose around – and I'd sooner shoot him than cage him."

"I know he wouldn't hurt anyone unless

they hurt him!" she cried. But Tom looked away with troubled face.

"You know how we would feel if there was an accident," he said.

"Well, don't do it yet — after dinner — not yet."

The evening meal passed in heavy silence. They were both thinking about what would have to be done. As they rose from the table the woman began to cry. She said: "Oh Tom, you can't!"

"I'll have to," said the man, still looking away from her. Suddenly she took his arm.

"Come and see him, before we make up our minds!"

They passed along the veranda to the old outside fireplace. Chut was lying on his back beside the faded and shredded remains of the trousers that had mothered him. His eyes were soft and sad with dreams.

As the man and woman looked down at him, he reached up great arms to catch his great toe.

With tears and laughter mingling in her voice, the woman said: "Oh, Tom, he can't be dangerous! Look at him!"

"He doesn't look it," said the man, tears gleaming in his eyes.

Just then the girl fell swiftly to her knees, her fingers searching the velvet fur just above the kangaroo's quivering nose. "Look!" she cried. "Look!"

The man held the lamp down. On Chut's nose there was a small, deep, raw pit, eaten into the flesh. About the edges of the rawness the hair was singed and burnt.

"Couldn't that have been done by a cigarette?" she questioned.

"You bet it was!" he replied.

"Well," she said, "that's *his* side of the story for you, Tom!" Then she reached down and clasped her arms about Chut's neck. "Oh, I am so glad! So glad!"

They stood up.

"I," said the man, "am sorry . . ."

"What do you *mean*?" questioned the girl.

"I'm sorry Chut's done such a good job with the yardman that he hasn't left me a chance!" said Tom Henton, his fingers lingering about the swell of his bicep.

Later the girl slipped back and gave Chut a whole half-loaf of bread with melted sugar. He ate it placidly and blissfully, with small tickings of pleasure. Sugar ran down his chin and got into his fur. He was soon perfectly horrible with sugar and covered with crumbs. Nevertheless, his mistress stooped and kissed him.

How the Turtle Got his Shell

A Story from New Guinea

John Yeoman

This is a story from the days when the animals were all what the Papuans call "bariawa", and spoke and behaved just as humans do now.

A long time ago, longer ago than any of us can remember, the turtle and the wallaby were friends. In those days the turtle had no shell and so he could move more quickly, and had no trouble trotting along behind his companion.

One afternoon, when they were sunning themselves on the beach, the turtle suddenly announced that he felt very hungry.

The wallaby thought a bit and then said, "I have an idea. Let's creep into Binama's garden and eat some of his sugar-cane and bananas. He'll never know."

The turtle was uncertain at first. Binama the hornbill had a ferocious temper and was proud of his garden – but the thought of sugar-cane and bananas was very tempting.

"All right, then," he said. "But we must be careful not to be seen."

They tiptoed across the sand to the gate and peered through the bars. There was no one about, so they let themselves in.

To make things easier for his friend, the wallaby trampled down the stems of the sugar-cane and bent the stalks of the bananas. They had never had such a feast.

Now, about this time all the birds were returning from their gardens with the taro-roots which they had dug up for their evening meal.

They gathered in the village compound and set about peeling the roots and cutting them up for the pot.

Suddenly Binama the hornbill said,

"Someone must go down to the beach to fetch some sea water for us to cook with. We want our taro to be nice and salty."

The birds secretly agreed, but no one offered to go. They were frightened that there might be some enemy lying in wait on the way.

One by one they invented excuses until finally the brave little wagtail put them all to shame by saying, "Well, if no one else is prepared to fetch the water, I suppose I shall have to go."

But he was taking no chances. Before he set out with his bottles he hung his shell breastplate round his neck, tied a bunch of waving feathers round his head and took up his spear.

And to make himself feel even safer he skipped from side to side as he made his way towards the beach – to confuse any enemy that might be lurking in the undergrowth.

When they caught sight of him bobbing along beside the hornbill's garden the wallaby and the turtle were overcome with fear. But the turtle managed to say, "Please don't be surprised to find us in your master's

garden. Binama was kind enough to invite us to help ourselves."

The wagtail was clever enough to pretend that he believed the turtle, and simply bowed before continuing on his way to the water's edge. But he knew that the turtle had not been telling the truth.

As soon as he had filled his bottles with sea water he skipped back to the village by another path, and told the other birds what he had seen.

"How dare the wallaby and the turtle steal

food from our master," they cried. "We'll soon put a stop to that!" And taking their spears they flocked down to Binama's garden and surrounded it.

When he saw what was happening the wallaby gave a tremendous leap which sent him soaring above their heads, and he bounded away into the bushes.

The unfortunate turtle could do nothing but scamper into the shelter of a yam patch, where the trembling leaves soon gave him away.

As the birds dragged him out he pleaded with them for mercy. "It wasn't my fault," he whimpered. "It was the wallaby who broke all the stalks down and . . ." But the birds weren't interested in his excuses and hauled him off to Binama's house. The hornbill ordered him to be tied up and put on a shelf until the following day.

The next morning Binama announced that there was to be a great feast at which they would slay the turtle, and he ordered all the birds to make preparations.

When the horrified turtle noticed that

everyone had gone out to the gardens to collect food and that only the young hornbills were left in the house to guard him, he decided on a plan.

"Sweet little masters," he said in a gentle voice, "if only you would be good enough to untie me, we could play a little game."

The young hornbills, not suspecting what was in his mind, undid the knots.

The turtle crawled down from the ledge, stretched his arms and legs a bit to relieve the cramps, and then said, "Shall we dress up? If you brought me all your best ornaments I could put them on."

The young hornbills eagerly showed him a basket full of Binama's most precious ornaments – a fine necklace of shell money, two shell armlets and a carved wooden bowl.

They helped the turtle to wind the necklace round his neck, and slip the armlets on to his arms, and fasten the bowl on his back.

"I must look a wonderful sight," said the turtle. "I'll trot around for a while to show you how your father looks when he's dressed in his finery."

The young hornbills watched him waddle a few paces before calling him back. He returned at once to the shade of the tree under which the young birds were sitting.

"Well?" he asked. "How do I look?"

In fact he looked so ridiculous that the little hornbills could hardly answer for laughing. They encouraged him to do it again, and he was more than pleased to oblige.

When the young birds heard the others returning they called out to the turtle to come back.

But it was too late. He had heard the others as well, and was making a dash for the shore.

The children at last realized what was happening and shouted, "Quick, quick; the turtle is escaping!"

The birds flung their bundles of food to the ground and set off after the turtle, but he had already reached the sea and plunged in.

Binama and the angry birds knew that he must come up for air. "Show yourself, turtle," they cried. "Lift up your head."

When the turtle came up for a breath, they hurled great stones at him, and one shattered his left armlet before he dived for safety.

"Show yourself turtle," they cried again. "Lift up your head."

When he came up for another breath, they hurled more stones and shattered his right armlet before he dived.

The third time they snapped the string of the necklace of shell money.

For the last time they cried, "Show yourself, turtle. Lift up your head." But no matter how many stones they rained down upon his back, they couldn't even make a dent in the solid wooden bowl.

In no time the turtle was out of sight, and an angry Binama led his followers back to the village.

And since then the turtle has always carried the hornbill's wooden bowl on his back.

Life With Tilly

Philippa Pearce

Ben Blewitt enjoys living in London – but he would also like to have a dog of his own. Grandfather Fitch mentioned giving Ben a dog for his birthday but when it turned out just to be a wool-stitched picture, Ben was bitterly disappointed. It is on his visits to his grandparents in the countryside that Ben can nearly believe that he has a dog. For there he looks after Tilly, his grandfather's spaniel. This is the story of one incident where Ben and Tilly have fun together – and where Ben finds out more about the elderly spaniel.

It wasn't that Ben wanted to live in the country – oh, no! The country was well enough for holidays and visits, but Ben was a

124

Londoner, like his father. Mr Blewitt was an Underground worker, and, as the only British Underground is in London, Mr Blewitt could no more live out of London than a fish could live out of water. Besides, he liked London; so did Ben.

Ben liked to rattle down moving staircases to platforms where subterranean winds wafted the coming of the trains; he liked to burrow along below London. Above ground, he liked to sail high on the tops of London buses, in the currents of traffic. He liked the feel of paving-stones hard beneath his feet, the streaming splendour of a wet night with all the lamps and lights shining and reflected, the smell of London. After all, London – a house in a row in a back-street just south of the river – was his home; and he had been called – so his father said – after Big Ben.

But he would have liked to have had a dog as well.

That was why Ben particularly enjoyed his country-visits to his grandparents. During a stay, Tilly became his. This was her own doing, and was done with delicacy, for she became his companion without ceasing to acknowledge Grandpa as her master.

Grandpa gave Tilly's care over to Ben. He made her dinner – kept an eye open for all rinds of bacon, for bones, and other left-overs including gravy, added dog-biscuit and a little water, and stewed it all up in Tilly's old enamel bowl on the kitchen-range. He combed out her spaniel curls, dusted her for fleas, gave her a condition powder – did everything. He shielded her from Mrs Fitch, who knew perfectly well that there was a dog about the place, and yet never allowed herself to become reconciled to the fact of it. Ben picked up Tilly's hairs whenever he saw them indoors, rubbed her feet on the doormat before he let her inside, and walked between her and his grandmother when they entered together. Young Tilly herself knew how to evade notice. In spite of her bulk – "a back made to carry a tea-tray," Grandpa said – she could move so lightly that there was not so much as a click of her toe-nails on the linoleum.

Tilly was with Ben, whatever he was doing.

On the first days of his visit, he spent most of his time about the house and garden, helping Grandpa. He kindled the fire in the range, fetched the milk from the milk-box at the end of the driftway, pumped the water, dug the potatoes, fed the fowls, and gathered the eggs. Always Tilly was with him. They spent one whole afternoon with Grandpa, helping to knock up a new hen-coop for a hen with a brood of very late chickens. The chicks ran over Tilly's outstretched paws as she dozed in the sun to the beat of Ben's hammer on the nails.

On other days they were more adventurous. Granny directed Grandpa to pack a lunch of sandwiches for Ben, and he went out after breakfast until nearly tea-time – with Tilly.

They went down the driftway. Once – in spite of everyone's saying there weren't any more, nowadays – they started a rabbit. Tilly threw herself into the chase, ears streaming behind her, until the rabbit began really to run. Then, intelligently, Tilly stopped.

Once, in a copse, they started a squirrel; and Tilly would not believe she had no possible chance of catching it. She thought it must fall.

Once they found an old rubber ball in a ditch: Tilly found it and Ben threw it for her, and they only lost it hours later, in a bed of nettles.

The weather became hot, and they bathed. Just before reaching the driftway bridge over the Say, they would strike off across marshland to the river. Tilly led the way, for bathing was her passion. The marsh grasses and reeds grew much taller than she was, so that every so often she reared herself up on her hind legs to see where she was going. She dropped down again to steer a more exact course, each time resuming movement with greater eagerness. As they neared the river, Tilly could smell it. Her pace quickened so that she took the last few yards at a low run, whining. She would never jump in, but entered the water still at a run, and only began swimming when she felt her body beginning to sink.

Tilly swam round and round, whining, while Ben undressed by a willow tree. He did

not bother to put on bathing trunks, for there was never anyone about. He dived in and swam, and Tilly threshed the water round him.

There was never anyone about – until the last day of Ben's visit. That day, the weather was stiflingly hot, and Ben and Young Tilly bathed in the morning to keep cool. Afterwards, they lay under the willow tree where, even in its shade, the heat dried fur and skin. They shared the lunch between them – hard-boiled eggs and thick cheese sandwiches, and a bottle of lemonade as an extra for Ben. That made the day seem even heavier and drowsier. They slept.

So not even Tilly was awake when the canoe appeared for the first time, coming out from under the driftway bridge. There were two boys and a little girl in it. Between the knees of the older, red-haired boy, who sat in the stern, was a dog: an upstanding-looking mongrel, mostly terrier perhaps. He glanced towards the bank where Ben and Tilly lay, but they were hidden by the grasses, asleep. No wind blew a scent from them. The canoe passed and went out of sight.

The boy and the dog slept on. Breezes began to blow the leaves of the willow tree, so that their silvery-green undersides showed light against a darkened sky. Great black clouds crept overhead. Except for the abrupt, shivering little breezes, the air was hot, still, heavy before the storm. Then a single raindrop splashed on Ben's bare shoulder. He woke, and his movement woke Tilly.

The oncoming storm tried its strength out with a few more big drops, and Ben began hurriedly to collect his clothes to dress. Tilly was shivering and whining round him, getting in his way. Then she fell silent, turning towards the river, alert. Ben looked where she was looking, and at once dropped down behind the screen of grasses. The canoe they had missed before was coming back. Seeing the dog in it, Ben put his fingers through Tilly's collar. She had stiffened, but was willing to remain still and quiet.

The canoe was hurrying to get home before the rain. The two boys were paddling with all their might, and – to leave the stern-man quite free – the dog had been sent forward into the bows. There he sat, in front of the little girl, looking ahead over the water and from side to side at the banks. This time, on one of his side glances, the dog saw or smelt Till. There was no doubt of it, and Ben felt Tilly, under his hand, quiver responsively. The dog stood up now to look better at the bank, and the boat rocked as he moved.

"What is it, Toby?" called the boy at the stern; and, from the way he spoke, Ben knew he must be the master of the dog. With a pang he knew it: the boy was not much older than he, he did not look much richer – even the canoe was old and shabby – but he lived in the country, where you could exercise a dog. So he had a dog.

The other boy in the canoe cried that they must not stop for anything Toby had seen on the bank – it was already beginning to rain quite heavily. The canoe sped on. As it went, the dog in the bows turned sideways and finally right round in order to continue looking at the place on the bank where Tilly was. Then the canoe disappeared under the bridge; and the rain was really coming down.

Then Tilly seemed to go mad. She raced up and down the bank, barking, and then flounced into the water, and swam round furiously, barking and snapping at the raindrops as though they were a new kind of fly. Ben had not meant to bathe again, but now, seeing Till in the poppling water, he could not resist. He dived in and swam under her, which always agitated her. He came up in a shallow, and stood with the raindrops fountaining in the water round him and beating on his head and shoulders and rushing down them. "Tilly! Tilly!" he shouted, for Tilly – now that the canoe had gone far off – was setting off in its pursuit, still barking. She heard Ben and turned, coming back with the same speed as in her going, and with such an impact on Ben's legs when she reached him that they both went down together into the water, their barking and shouting almost drowned in the rushing of water and wind.

Thunder was rolling up, with lightning. They went ashore. Ben pulled on his clothes, and they began to run home. The marshland was becoming a slough; the driftway was becoming a marsh. Black clouds darkened their muddy way; lightning lit it. By the time they reached the refuge of their home-porch, water seemed to be descending from the sky in continuous volume instead of in separate raindrops.

Ben stumbled in through the front door. A pathway of newspapers had been laid from its threshold to the scullery. "Straight through to a hot bath," called Mrs Fitch;

"and that dog's too wet and muddy for a decent home."

"She's not; and she's frightened of lightning," said Ben. The violence of the storm excused contradiction. He picked up Tilly and carried her along the paper-way into the scullery, his grandmother no longer protesting. In the scullery Grandpa was pouring cans of hot water into a tin bath. He winked when he saw Young Tilly, and fetched a clean sack to rub her down.

Ben had his hot bath, and towelled himself, and Grandpa gave him his dry change of clothes. The rain was streaming in wide rivers down the scullery window. "We bathed in it, Grandpa," said Ben, "as we were going to be caught in it, anyway." He remembered the hurrying canoe, and described it and its occupants.

"The red-headed one'll be young Codling," said Grandpa, "and the others must be Bob Moss's two youngest."

"And the dog? Does he belong to the red-haired boy?"

"Aye."

"Tilly was frightened of him."

"Of young Codling?"

"No, of his dog."

"She's a sly one," said Grandpa emphatically, closing one eye. "That Toby fathered her puppies some two years back. But she's too old for such tricks now."

Ben sighed. Young Tilly's mother, Old Tilly, had been old when she had had her last litter of puppies, of which Young Tilly had been one; but Young Tilly was now even older than Old Tilly had been then.

The storm continued, and during tea there was a particularly violent outburst. Young Mrs Perkins, sheltering under a raincoat, dashed in from next door to ask, "You all right?" She said excitedly that this was the worst storm her husband could remember. Granny was saying that the importance of that remark depended upon how far back a person could remember, and that depended upon his age, which might be nothing to speak of. But Mrs Perkins was already dashing home again.

Up to now, Tilly had been hiding under the

furniture; now she made a rush to get out through the door after Mrs Perkins. On the very threshold she darted back from a flash of lightning that, branched like a tree, seemed to hang in the sky, ghastly, for seconds. She yelped and fled back again to the shelter of Grandpa's chair. She squeezed under it so far that she stuck, and the old man had to get up to release her.

"Fat, and a coward," said Granny.

Everyone knew that Tilly was – well, timid, yet she wanted to go out, even in this thunderstorm. She spent all that evening crawling towards the front door, and then dashing back in terror. For the storm continued with lightning, thunder, and floods of rain.

How the Cat Became

Ted Hughes

Things were running very smoothly and most of the creatures were highly pleased with themselves. Lion was already famous. Even the little shrews and moles and spiders were pretty well known.

But among all these busy creatures there was one who seemed to be getting nowhere. It was Cat.

Cat was a real oddity. The others didn't know what to make of him at all.

He lived in a hollow tree in the wood. Every night, when the rest of the creatures were sound asleep, he retired to the depths of his tree – then such sounds, such screechings, yowlings, wailings! The bats that slept upside-down all day long in the hollows of the tree branches awoke with a start and fled with their wing-tips stuffed into their ears. It seemed to them that Cat was having the worst nightmares ever – ten at a time.

But no. Cat was tuning his violin.

If only you could have seen him! Curled in the warm smooth hollow of his tree, gazing up through the hole at the top of the trunk, smiling at the stars, winking at the moon – his violin tucked under his chin. Ah, Cat was a happy one.

And all night long he sat there composing his tunes.

Now the creatures didn't like this at all. They saw no use in his music, it made no food, it built no nest, it didn't even keep him warm. And the way Cat lounged around all day, sleeping in the sun, was just more than they could stand.

"He's a bad example," said Beaver, "he never does a stroke of work! What if our children think they can live as idly as he does?"

"It's time," said Weasel, "that Cat had a job like everybody else in the world."

So the creatures of the wood formed a

Committee to persuade Cat to take a job.

Jay, Magpie, and Parrot went along at dawn and sat in the topmost twigs of Cat's old tree. As soon as Cat poked his head out, they all began together:

"You've to get a job. Get a job! Get a job!"

That was only the beginning of it. All day long, everywhere he went, those birds were at him:

"Get a job! Get a job!"

And try as he would, Cat could not get one wink of sleep.

That night he went back to his tree early. He was far too tired to practise on his violin and fell fast asleep in a few minutes. Next morning, when he poked his head out of the tree at first light, the three birds of the Committee were there again, loud as ever:

"Get a job!"

Cat ducked back down into his tree and began to think. He wasn't going to start grubbing around in the wet woods all day, as they wanted him to. Oh no. He wouldn't have any time to play his violin if he did that. There was only one thing to do and he did it.

He tucked his violin under his arm and suddenly jumped out at the top of the tree and set off through the woods at a run. Behind him, shouting and calling, came Jay, Magpie, and Parrot.

Other creatures that were about their daily work in the undergrowth looked up when Cat ran past. No one had ever seen Cat run before.

"Cat's up to something," they called to each other. "Maybe he's going to get a job at last."

Deer, Wild Boar, Bear, Ferret, Mongoose, Porcupine, and a cloud of birds set off after Cat to see where he was going.

After a great deal of running they came to the edge of the forest. There they stopped. As they peered through the leaves they looked sideways at each other and trembled. Ahead of them, across an open field covered with haycocks, was Man's farm.

But Cat wasn't afraid. He went straight on, over the field, and up to Man's door. He raised his paw and banged as hard as he could in the middle of the door.

Man was so surprised to see Cat that at first he just stood, eyes wide, mouth open. No creature ever dared to come on to his fields, let alone knock at his door. Cat spoke first.

"I've come for a job," he said.

"A job?" asked Man, hardly able to believe his ears.

"Work," said Cat. "I want to earn my living."

Man looked him up and down, then saw his long claws.

"You look as if you'd make a fine rat-catcher," said Man.

Cat was surprised to hear that. He wondered what it was about him that made him look like a rat-catcher. Still, he wasn't going to miss the chance of a job. So he stuck out his chest and said: "Been doing it for years."

"Well then, I've a job for you," said Man. "My farm's swarming with rats and mice. They're in my haystacks, they're in my corn sacks, and they're all over the pantry."

So before Cat knew where he was, he had been signed on as a Rat-and-Mouse-Catcher. His pay was milk, and meat, and a place at the fireside. He slept all day and worked all night.

At first he had a terrible time. The rats pulled his tail, the mice nipped his ears. They climbed on to rafters above him and dropped down – thump! on to him in the dark. They teased the life out of him.

But Cat was a quick learner. At the end of the week he could lay out a dozen rats and twice as many mice within half an hour. If he'd gone on laying them out all night there would pretty soon have been none left, and Cat would have been out of a job. So he just caught a few each night – in the first ten minutes or so. Then he retired into the barn and played his violin till morning. This was just the job he had been looking for.

Man was delighted with him. And Mrs Man thought he was beautiful. She took him on to her lap and stroked him for hours on end. What a life! thought Cat. If only those silly creatures in the dripping wet woods could see him now!

Well, when the other farmers saw what a fine rat-and-mouse-catcher Cat was, they all wanted cats too. Soon there were so many cats that our Cat decided to form a string

band. Oh yes, they were all great violinists. Every night, after making one pile of rats and another of mice, each cat left his farm and was away over the fields to a little dark spinney.

Then what tunes! All night long . . .

Pretty soon lady cats began to arrive. Now, every night, instead of just music, there was dancing too. And what dances! If only you could have crept up there and peeped into the glade from behind a tree and seen the cats dancing – the glossy furred ladies and the tomcats, some pearly grey, some ginger red, and all with wonderful green flashing eyes. Up and down the glade, with the music flying out all over the night.

At dawn they hung their violins in the larch trees, dashed back to the farms, and pretended they had been working all night among the rats and mice. They lapped their milk hungrily, stretched out at the fireside, and fell asleep with smiles on their faces.

Wandering Prince

Gordon Snell

The circus was quiet now. In the hazy moonlight, the big tent and the caravans looked like a group of huge, strange animals crouching in the field. An owl hooted in the forest nearby. The only other sound was a steady munching, as Prince the pony chewed the grass around the tree he was tied to.

Prince was pleased with himself: the evening's show had been a big success, and Prince was sure that he had been the star attraction. The audience clapped loudly when he came prancing in, with his red bridle and the spray of bright feathers on his head. They were delighted when he stood on his hind legs and walked round the ring, and when he trotted round and round with Laura, the acrobat, standing on one leg on his back.

He was sure they had liked him more than any of the other acts: more than Chapman the ringmaster, with his twirly moustaches, red coat and crackling whip; more than his daughter, Laura, swinging – on the high trapeze or walking on the tightrope; more than Laura's husband, Dan, with his knife-throwing and sword-swallowing; more even than Bobo the Clown, who kept falling over and spilling buckets of water on himself; and certainly the audience liked him more than the only other animals in the show – Dilly and Dally, the Performing Pekinese. Prince thought they were very silly, with their fancy ribbons and their ladder-climbing act, and their yapping in time to music.

So, as he munched away at the grass in the moonlight, Prince looked forward to the two performances Chapman's Circus were going to give tomorrow at this little town beside the New Forest, and he smiled as he thought of the cheers and applause to come.

Suddenly Prince stopped munching, and lifted his head, listening. He had the feeling he was being watched. He turned, and saw a face gazing at him from the trees at the edge of the forest. It was another pony.

The two ponies stared at each other for more than a minute, without moving. Then the newcomer walked slowly out from the trees and across the field, towards Prince. He was one of the wild ponies that live in the New Forest, and he was brown and tough-looking, with a shaggy mane and tail that had clearly never been trimmed and groomed like Prince's. The Forest pony stopped a few yards away, and again the two of them stared at each other for a while. Then the Forest pony turned his head away, and began munching the grass. Prince didn't know quite what to do, so he started munching too, now and then glancing warily at the other pony.

"Where did you spring from, then?"

Prince was startled by the sudden, sharp question: but he didn't want to show it.

"Circus," he said, trying to sound gruff.

The Forest pony grunted, and went on chewing the grass. After a couple of minutes he looked up and said, in the same

147

challenging tone: "What's your name, then?"

"Prince."

"Prince, eh?" The Forest pony made a noise that sounded very like a chuckle of laughter. Prince was annoyed.

"What's yours?" he said, trying to sound bolder than he really felt.

The Forest pony stared at Prince for a bit, then said, "Joe," and went back to his chewing. Prince did the same. Then Joe spoke again.

"What do you do, in the circus?"

Prince could sense that behind the rather sneering tone of the question, Joe was really curious to know. He felt that here was his chance to get the upper hand.

"Oh, this and that," he said, casually. "I walk on my hind legs, as a matter of fact. I wear feathers on my head, and a red bridle. I trot round, balancing a lady on my back. I snatch the clown's hat and he chases me. Then I throw it into the audience . . ."

Prince stopped. He could hardly believe his ears. Joe was laughing. Laughing at *him*. Prince was furious.

"What's so funny?" he snarled.

"You do all that?" asked Joe, still chuckling. "Hind legs . . . feathers . . . balancing ladies . . . throwing hats about . . .?"

"Certainly I do," said Prince.

"Whatever for?"

The question completely stumped Prince. He had never asked himself *why* he did his circus act. He had never met anyone who *didn't* think it was clever – and now here was this scruffy character from the Forest, actually laughing with scorn at his skills.

"I bet you couldn't do all that," said Prince, huffily.

"Wouldn't want to," said Joe. "I'd rather do pony-things, not silly tricks to amuse humans, like some performing dog."

This really stung Prince's pride. Was Joe comparing *him* to idiotic creatures like Dilly and Dally? He snorted with rage – and the faint suspicion that Joe might perhaps be right made him angrier still. He snorted again, and pawed the ground, and charged, head down, at Joe. But the rope pulled him up, just out of range, and he stood there,

149

pawing and snarling and baring his teeth.

"That's more like it!" said Joe. "Now you're acting like a real pony!"

Prince stopped snarling, and his anger faded away. He found he was rather pleased at Joe's approval. He tossed his head, and whinnied.

"Of course I'm a real pony," he said. "What did you think I was? A crocodile?" Joe laughed.

"Come on then, Prancing Prince," he said. "Let's go!"

Prince was taken aback.

"Go? Go where?" he asked.

"Into the forest, of course," said Joe.

Prince didn't like the idea. The forest looked dark and threatening. But he couldn't admit that to Joe. Luckily, though, he had the perfect excuse.

"I'd love to go," he said, "but I can't. I'm tied to the tree."

"No problem," said Joe. "What do you think teeth are for?" And he promptly started chewing at the rope.

"Wait," said Prince. "I don't really want . . .

that is, I don't think we should . . ."

Joe was impatient.

"You want to get free, don't you? Well, start chewing!" He went on biting at the rope, and there was nothing Prince could do but start biting, too. It wasn't long before the rope began to fray, and soon only a thin thread connected one part of it to the other.

"Go on – now – pull!" said Joe.

Reluctantly, Prince pulled. The rope snapped. He was free. But did he really want to be? Prince wasn't at all sure.

"Come on then!" called Joe. "Follow me!" And he trotted off into the shadowy trees of the forest. Prince looked around. He would have been quite pleased if Mr Chapman had come storming out of his caravan, swearing, and tied him up again. But the field was quiet, and there was no one to stop him going. If he stayed where he was, Joe would come back and mock at him. He couldn't bear that – so off he went, walking timidly into the forest.

All around him were tall trees. They seemed to Prince like a crowd of giants, waiting and watching. A breeze stirred the leaves above his head, and the patterns of moonlight on the forest floor rippled like water. Somewhere among the shadows, an owl hooted. Prince's hoofs made a crunching noise as he walked on the dry brushwood and leaves. Some way ahead he could see the dark shape of Joe, who had stopped and was looking back at him.

"Come on," said Joe, and he started trotting, on a zigzagging path among the trees. Prince followed: he didn't want to lose sight of Joe, so he dodged and darted behind him through the Forest, with the branches brushing against him.

Joe stopped, and Prince came to a halt beside him, panting. They were at the edge of the trees now, looking out on to a stretch of heathland, with a rough carpet of heather and clumps of bushes here and there. After the gloom of the forest, the heath was silvery bright in the moonlight.

Prince was thankful: he'd be glad to be out in the open again. But then he saw there was a fence between them and the heath. There was a five-barred wooden gate in it, nearly as high as Prince's neck; and the gate was closed.

"Ready to jump?" asked Joe.

At first, Prince thought he must be joking. The only jumps he had ever made were in the circus, when Bobo the Clown held a pole out for him, a foot or so above the ground. This gate must be over three times as high. But Joe was serious.

"Up and over, Prince!" he said – and he rushed towards the gate, leapt into the air, and landed on the far side. He looked back at Prince.

"Come on, it's easy," he said, "and more fun than capering about in that circus."

Prince walked slowly back, away from the gate, and then turned. He took a deep breath, and charged. The gate loomed up in front of him. He closed his eyes and pushed his back feet hard on the ground, reaching up, up into the air with his front legs. For a moment, he seemed to be flying like a bird: it was a marvellous feeling. Then the ground was rushing up towards him, and his front feet landed with a thud. He stumbled, recovered his balance, and stood still. He lifted his head in the air and whinnied with delight and relief. He'd done it!

Joe whinnied, too.

"Nice work," he said. "I never thought you'd make it."

"Whatever made you think that?" said Prince. He felt very proud of himself – but things didn't turn out to be quite as easy as he expected . . .

"What next?" he asked Joe.

"Racing," said Joe. "Bet you can't catch me!" He began to trot, and then to canter, across the heath. Prince managed to keep up with him for a couple of minutes, but he was getting tired. A short spell of trotting was all he was used to in the circus.

"I'm not as fit as I ought to be," he thought to himself. "Must try to get more exercise in future . . ."

"Away we go!" shouted Joe, and now he began to gallop over the heath, towards a wood on the far side. Prince pounded after him, but the gap between them was getting bigger. Joe must have been more than a hundred yards away when Prince saw him reach the wood and go galloping on into the trees. Panting heavily, he got to the place where Joe had gone into the wood. All he could see was a maze of leaves and shadows. Which way had Joe gone? Prince peered into the wood, and listened. He could hear nothing. The trees seemed simply to have swallowed Joe up. Prince was worried. If he went in there, he might get lost and never find his way out again. If he went back across the heath, would he ever find the gate they had jumped – let alone be able to jump back over it again? And even if he did that, how would he find his way back through the dark forest? Prince was miserable. He just stood there, not knowing what to do.

Suddenly the silence was broken by a sound that nearly made him jump into the air with fright. It was a sort of grunting, wailing roar, and it sounded anything but friendly. He turned round. There on the heath, just a little distance away, was a huge creature with a tall head, and antlers like mad, spiky television aerials. It was a red deer. Behind him Prince could see a group of smaller deer, some grazing, others looking up to see what their leader was making such a row about.

The big deer roared again, then put his head down, and started running towards Prince.

Then Prince had an idea. He stood up on his hind legs, just like he did in the circus. Then he lifted his head and neighed loudly.

The big deer stopped in his tracks, like a car screeching to a halt. He looked up at Prince, and his mouth dropped open in amazement.

Prince was still scared: he couldn't walk on his hind legs for all that long. He'd have to come down soon, and what would the deer do then? The big creature was still staring at him. Just as Prince felt that he'd have to give up, he heard a voice behind him. It was Joe.

"It's all right, Thunderhead, he's a friend of mine."

"Well, tell him he shouldn't dance about like that – it's not natural," said Thunderhead, and he walked away.

"Sorry I wasn't around when he showed up," said Joe, "I thought you were following me into the wood. Then when I stopped, and you weren't there, I came back to find you."

"Thanks," said Prince. "I couldn't have stood up like that for much longer."

"You must teach me that trick – it could come in useful."

"I'd be pleased to."

Prince was delighted to have Joe's approval.

"Now, let me show you around a bit more," said Joe. 'There's lots we haven't seen yet." They walked together into the wood.

The dawn was coming now, and the dark shapes of the trees were beginning to get back their daylight colours. The air was cool and fresh, and full of delicious smells, quite different from the circus smells Prince was used to: sawdust, and canvas, and leather, and diesel fumes from the trucks and the generator. Here in the wood, the soft breeze carried the scents of many flowers, and there was a clean, damp smell from the old leaves scattered on the ground.

They came to a busy stream, and waded in and drank the cold, refreshing water. Crossing the stream, they came out of the wood into a wide field of grass, and galloped around it, just for the joy of running. They rolled about on the grass, kicking their legs in the air. Then they lay down and dozed in the sunshine.

"The circus!" Prince said. "I'll be late for the afternoon show!" He nudged Joe who woke up, blinking in the sunlight.

"Joe – I've got to get back to the circus."

"Why?"

Prince found the question hard to answer.

"Well . . . they'll be expecting me. I'll be late . . ."

"Let them wait," said Joe. "And anyway, why go back at all? It's a good life here. Stay in the forest. I've got so much to show you."

Prince felt a glow of pleasure: Joe wanted to be his friend. He would like to say yes, he'd stay. But could he really leave the circus, and all the applause, and the travelling from place to place? Then Prince realized that although he'd travelled all over the country, he'd really *seen* very little: just fields that were very much alike, and the same circus tent, and the inside of the rattly old horsebox he travelled in. In fact, he'd seen more and learned more in his few hours in the forest with Joe than he had in all his travels with Mr Chapman. And yet . . .

"I'd better go, Joe," he said, sadly. "They'll come out looking for me, and *make* me go back."

"Well, if that's how you feel, there's not much I can do about it." Joe sounded hurt. "Come on."

Joe led the way back through the wood and across the heath. This time he gave no words of praise when Prince managed to jump the gate again. Back they went, through the forest trees, saying nothing. They stopped at the edge of the forest, and looked at the field with the circus tent in it. There was a lot of activity going on now – music was playing, and Bobo the Clown was standing outside the tent, ringing a bell, and shouting: "Roll up! Roll up!"

Just then, Mr Chapman and Laura came round the side of the tent. Mr Chapman was shouting angrily.

"Ten minutes to go, and still no sign of him! I should never have let *you* tie him up! Now look what's happened! No pony!"

"I tied him up all right," said Laura tearfully. "But he chewed through the rope . . ."

"From now on we'll put him on a chain," said Mr Chapman. "*And* I'll cut his rations!"

Prince nearly turned round right then – but he noticed that Laura was crying. She had always been fond of him, and petted him, and given him lumps of sugar. The rest of them couldn't care less, thought Prince: to them, he was just a stupid pony that did tricks and helped to bring in the money. He didn't want Laura to take the blame.

Prince made up his mind: he had a plan all worked out now. He said to Joe:

"Come and see the show tonight. There's a narrow gap in the tent at the back there, and you can peep through."

"I might," said Joe.

"Please do – *please*. It's important."

"OK," said Joe. "It'll be a chance to say goodbye, anyway."

Yes, thought Prince. Tonight, after the show, the circus would pack up and move off to somewhere miles away.

Joe turned and walked off into the forest. Prince watched him go. Then he walked smartly out into the circus field.

"There he is!" shouted Mr Chapman, grabbing Prince roughly by his mane. "Where have you been, you four-legged fool? I'll teach you to go running off like that!" And he gave Prince a slap on the side of his head.

"Don't!" said Laura.

"Get that beast's bridle on at once! We've only two minutes before the show starts!"

He went stamping off, and Laura put on Prince's red bridle with the feathers on top. Usually, he felt good in it – but now he thought it made him look rather foolish.

Prince went through all his tricks as usual, and the audience clapped and cheered. But he found that he didn't like the sound much, any more. He was thinking of the sound the birds made, in their dawn chorus in the wood, and the sound of the splashing stream, and the sound of his hoofs, and Joe's, as they crunched the dry forest floor.

When the afternoon show had finished, Mr Chapman said: "Right! Lock that pony in his horsebox! I'm not having him escaping again."

So Prince spent the two hours until the next show standing in his cramped, dark box.

At the evening show he trotted round obediently as usual, while Mr Chapman cracked his whip. Then, up he went on his hind legs, and pranced about, while the audience clapped. He glanced towards the gap in the far side of the tent, and there was Joe's face, gazing in.

No one in the circus tent was ready for what happened next. Prince started walking slowly towards Chapman. He backed away.

"That's enough, Prince – good boy, Prince," he said nervously.

Prince leaned forward and snatched the whip out of his hand. He chewed on it, and the handle broke into pieces. Prince dropped them on the sawdust floor, and bowed. The audience laughed and clapped loudly: they thought this was part of the act. But Mr Chapman didn't laugh: he was snarling.

"Get out! The act's over! Get out of the ring!"

Prince took no notice. He reached his mouth up towards Mr Chapman's head, and snatched with his teeth, grabbing the ringmaster's black hair. The hair came away – the whole lot of it! It was a wig. Mr Chapman stood there with his bald head gleaming under the bright lights. The audience were delighted. They shouted and clapped and stamped their feet.

Mr Chapman, his face red with rage, made a grab at Prince, who started to trot round the ring with Mr Chapman chasing him. Prince's pace got quicker as the ringmaster panted along behind him. Then, he stopped suddenly, and rose on his hind legs; Mr Chapman ran straight into him, and fell over. The crowd cheered.

Prince took a bow, trotted out of the tent and round to the back, where Joe was.

"Come on!" said Prince. As they trotted away together into the forest, Prince glanced back and saw Mr Chapman in the entrance to the tent, shouting and shaking his fist. Behind him stood Laura, smiling. She gave a goodbye wave.

The ponies ran through the forest, crashing against branches as they went. They jumped the gate, and ran out on to the heath, the way they'd come the night before. They ran into the wood on the far side, and then stopped and listened. All they could hear was the rustle of leaves in the night breeze, and the far-off hooting of the owl. No one seemed to be following.

They smiled at each other.

"That was quite a show!" said Joe admiringly.

"It wasn't bad, was it, for a farewell performance?" said Prince.

"You're not going back, then?" asked Joe.

"Never!" said Prince. "I'm retiring from the circus! This is the life for me!" And he lay on the ground and kicked his legs in the air for sheer joy. Then he felt something between his head and the ground, and realized he still had his bridle on. He sat up, dismayed.

"The bridle!" he said to Joe. "I can't go round the forest with this on my head, and the feathers too. It looks ridiculous. Help me get it off."

With Prince telling him what to do, Joe began to pull at the buckles and straps with his teeth. Finally, the bridle slipped off and fell on the ground. Prince tossed his head and shook himself. He was free.

"Thanks, Joe."

"It's a pleasure. Welcome to the forest."

In reply, Prince raised his head and gave a loud whinny. Joe whinnied back. Then Prince picked up the bridle in his teeth, and hung it on the low branch of a tree.

The two ponies walked slowly away through the wood, in the dappled moonlight. Prince turned once, and looked back at the bridle, hanging in the tree. The coloured feathers made it look as if some strange, bright bird had perched there.

The Crocodile and
the Monkey

Rose Fyleman

There was once a crocodile who lived on a
sandbank in a river. He was quite a nice
fellow, sociable and affectionate, though not
very clever. His wife, on the other hand, was
not at all a nice person. She was, I am sorry to
tell you, cruel, selfish and vain, and of a very
jealous disposition. In spite of this, her husband adored her. He even made poems to her.

They weren't particularly good poems; but
it isn't very easy to make good poems, as
everyone knows who has tried. But they
weren't bad, for a crocodile. And I told you he
wasn't very brainy. Here is one of the poems
he made:

My beauteous one, my dear beauteous one
My croco – croco dear,
By land or sea, where e'er it be
You have no single peer.

Your graceful form, your melting eyes,
My loving heart beguile,
I've searched around, no charm I've found
To match your darling smile.

When he told this to his wife she didn't look as pleased as you might have expected.

"I don't like that last bit," she said; "the bit about searching around."

"No, I don't think that is a very good bit," said her husband. "I had a lot of difficulty over the last line but one. It sounds a little awkward, doesn't it? It wouldn't flow."

"I don't mind about the flow," said his wife. "It's the searching around I don't like, I tell you. You've no business to be searching around for a better smile than mine."

It was no use her husband trying to explain that he put that in to make a rhyme. Mrs Crocodile wouldn't look at it that way, and though he changed the lines to:

> *But oh, how fair, how sweet and rare*
> *Your darling, darling smile.*

that made no difference. She kept on brooding over it and turning it over in her mind long after he had forgotten all about it.

The crocodile's wife was a lazy creature; she never moved about much, but spent most of her time idly basking in the sun and admiring her own reflection in the water. The crocodile, though, was rather energetic, and would go quite a long way in search of adventure. She always made him tell her exactly where he had been – he had to give an account of every single minute. This he always did most faithfully and truly, for he really had a very sincere nature.

One day, on one of his expeditions, he came to a place in the river where a fine banyan tree stood on the bank. He was hot and tired, and he lay down in the shallow water near the bank and rested. The banyan tree cast a pleasant shade, which he found very agreeable. Presently he noticed a monkey in the branches of the tree busy picking and eating the ripe fruit.

"Good morning," said the crocodile, when the monkey came down to a lower branch within speaking distance; "you seem to be enjoying yourself."

"Good morning to you, sir," replied the monkey. "I'm enjoying myself very much indeed. Would you like some fruit? There's plenty here for both of us."

The crocodile thanked him politely, and the monkey threw down some of the ripe fruit for him to eat. They had a little more amiable conversation, and then the crocodile bade the monkey farewell and went off home to his wife, to whom, as usual, he told the story of his morning's adventure.

Before many days had gone by he went again to the same spot and again saw the monkey in the banyan tree. This he felt to be very fortunate, as he had so much enjoyed meeting him before. They had another pleasant talk, and again the crocodile very much appreciated the fruit which the monkey threw down to him. It was indeed a very great treat, for crocodiles, being unable to climb trees, are not able to get fruit for themselves.

When the time came for the crocodile to depart, the monkey said he hoped they would meet again.

"I am generally here in the mornings," he said, "and shall always be delighted to see you."

The crocodile promised to come again soon, which he did, and so, in a short time quite a warm friendship sprang up between the two.

The crocodile told his new friend all about his lovely wife, and the monkey on several occasions sent her a present of banyan fruit. The monkey told the crocodile all about his own affairs and his many adventures among the forest trees, which could be seen not very far away, and what with one thing and another they spent many happy hours together.

But as time went on the crocodile's wife became suspicious of this new friendship.

"I've searched around" – she kept repeating over and over again to herself. "That's what he's been doing – searching around. I don't believe a word of what he says. Probably that monkey doesn't even exist. He's spending his time with someone else!"

She gradually worked herself up into a great state over this, but, being a cunning as well as a jealous creature, she decided not to tell her husband her thoughts until she had contrived some means of putting an end to this friendship of which she was so suspicious. Finally she decided on a plan, and as a first step she pretended to be very ill; so one day, when her husband came home, he found her lying on the sandbank groaning and lamenting.

He was, of course, very much upset by this. He was afraid his beautiful and adored wife was going to die. She was, by the way, a very good actress and certainly had every appearance of being very ill indeed. He suggested all sorts of remedies, but she would have none of them.

At last, when he was in utter despair, she said, interrupting her remarks with many groans, that she had once heard a very learned person say that the heart of a monkey was a certain cure for that very malady from which she was suffering.

"But how am I to procure such a thing?" asked the anxious husband.

"That is easy enough," said his groaning wife. "What about your friend in the banyan tree? You could easily persuade him to give you his heart if you put your mind to it."

Her husband was horrified at the suggestions as well he might be. Moreover, he was quite sure that the monkey would never consent to give him his heart, and said so. But his artful wife had a plan all ready in her head.

"There is no need at all for you to let him know that you want his heart," she said, "since you love me so little that you do not care to ask him for it. If you do as I tell you we can get him to come here without any difficulty, and once he is here and in our power we can do with him what we will."

The crocodile was more upset than ever when he heard his wife's cunning suggestion as to how the monkey was to be tricked into coming. He spoke of the kind way in which the monkey had always behaved and pointed out with great earnestness that nothing in the whole world was so hateful as the betrayal of a friend. But his wife would not listen to him. She was determined to put an end to this business and to destroy this rival, whoever it might be.

She groaned and moaned and rolled about and wept bitterly, declaring that he loved his friend better than his wife, and that he would be glad if she died so that he could be more free to spend his time with the monkey.

"You have been searching around," she said. "I guessed it some time ago and now I know it for certain. It is that which has made me fall a victim to this terrible illness. But you do not care. You no longer love me, that is the truth of the matter. Oh . . . oh . . . You will not have much longer to wait. Oh – oh – oh . . ." And she writhed about in apparent agony.

The poor crocodile was at his wits' end. What could he do? He still adored his horrid wife, strange though it seems, and he really believed she was terribly ill.

So at last, very reluctantly, and with many

misgivings, he promised to do what she wished. She thereupon gave him careful instructions as to how he must act in order to get the monkey to visit them, and he set off with a heavy heart.

The monkey was in the banyan tree as usual, happily jumping from branch to branch in the hot sunshine. When they had exchanged greetings and had had a little more pleasant talk, the crocodile felt that he could put off the evil moment no longer.

"I have a message for you from my wife," he said at last. "I have told her so much about you that she is dying to meet you. Moreover, she says I have been sadly wanting in hospitality never to have asked you to come and see us after your great kindness in the matter of the fruit. Will you not come back with me today and pay us a visit?"

"That is very kind of you," said the monkey, "and I should very much like to meet your wife, who, if she is as lovely as your description of her, must indeed be beautiful. But how am I to accompany you? I cannot swim; also I believe your home is in the water and I cannot breathe under water."

"That is quite easy," said the crocodile, "we live on a sandbank, where you will be quite comfortable. As for getting there, you have only to get on my back and I will convey you."

So the monkey accepted.

The crocodile's heart grew heavier and heavier. He was touched at the monkey's trust in him, which he was about to requite so hatefully. At the same time he kept thinking of his sick wife and how she would certainly die if he returned without the monkey.

The worst thing of all, it seemed to him, was the fact that the monkey would have to die without preparing as he should to meet his Maker.

He swam silently down the river, and the monkey, noticing this, asked him what he was thinking about. So then, feeling that the monkey could not possibly escape, for the river was wide and he kept well to the middle of it, he told him of the fate in store for him.

The monkey listened quietly until the crocodile had finished and then replied: "My dear friend, I have heard your tale with great sympathy and am very much touched by your unhappy situation. Willingly will I give you my heart in order to save the life of so beautiful a creature as your wife. But it is a pity you did not tell me before we started on this journey. I have a habit of hanging my heart every morning early on a branch of the banyan tree so that it should not get damaged while I am jumping about. However, the matter can easily be put right. If you will turn round and take me back I will get my heart for you."

So the crocodile, after earnestly thanking the monkey, swam back again to the place whence they had started. And as soon as they drew in to the bank the monkey leaped off the crocodile's back and up into the tree, and looked down at the crocodile, who was expectantly waiting close to the bank.

"Go back to your horrid wife, you silly old crocodile," said the monkey, "and tell her that monkeys may keep their hearts hanging on branches, but they keep their wits in their heads."

Escape

E.B. White

When Wilbur the piglet was born he was the smallest and weakest of the litter, so the farmer, Mr Arable, allowed his daughter, Fern, to look after Wilbur in the farmhouse. She fed him from a bottle, and as he grew he moved out of the house and into the orchard. When he was about five weeks old, arrangements were made for Wilbur to live at the Zuckermans', just down the road from Fern ...

The barn was very large. It was very old. It smelled of hay and it smelled of manure. It smelled of the perspiration of tired horses and the wonderful sweet breath of patient cows. It often had a sort of peaceful smell – as though nothing bad could happen ever again in the world. It smelled of grain and of harness dressing and of axle grease and of rubber boots and of new rope. And whenever the cat was given a fish-head to eat, the barn would smell of fish. But mostly it smelled of hay, for there was always hay in the great loft up overhead. And there was always hay being pitched down to the cows and the horses and the sheep.

The barn was pleasantly warm in winter when the animals spent most of their time indoors, and it was pleasantly cool in summer when the big doors stood wide open to the breeze. The barn had stalls on the main floor for the work horses, tie-ups on the main floor for the cows, a sheepfold down below for the sheep, a pigpen down below for Wilbur, and it was full of all sorts of things that you find in barns: ladders, grindstones, pitchforks, monkey wrenches, scythes, lawnmowers, snow shovels, axe handles, milk pails, water buckets, empty grain sacks, and rusty rat-traps. It was the kind of barn that swallows like to build their nests in. It was the kind of barn that children like to play in. And the whole thing was owned by Fern's uncle, Mr Homer L. Zuckerman.

Wilbur's new home was in the lower part of the barn, directly underneath the cows. Mr Zuckerman knew that a manure pile is a good place to keep a young pig. Pigs needed warmth, and it was warm and comfortable down there in the barn cellar on the south side.

Fern came, almost every day, to visit him. She found an old milking stool that had been discarded, and she placed the stool in the sheepfold next to Wilbur's pen. Here she sat quietly during the long afternoons, thinking and listening and watching Wilbur. The sheep soon got to know her and trust her. So did the geese, who lived with the sheep. All the animals trusted her, she was so quiet and friendly. Mr Zuckerman did not allow her to take Wilbur out, and he did not allow her to get into the pigpen. But he told Fern that she could sit on the stool and watch Wilbur as long as she wanted to. It made her happy just to be near the pig, and it made Wilbur happy to know that she was sitting there, right outside his pen. But he never had any fun – no walks, no rides, no swims.

One afternoon in June, when Wilbur was almost two months old, he wandered out into his small yard outside the barn. Fern had not arrived for her usual visit. Wilbur stood in the sun feeling lonely and bored.

"There's never anything to do round here," he thought. He walked slowly to his food trough and sniffed to see if anything had been overlooked at lunch. He found a small strip of potato skin and ate it. His back itched, so he leaned against the fence and rubbed against the boards. When he tired of this, he walked indoors, climbed to the top of the manure pile, and sat down. He didn't feel like going to sleep, he didn't feel like digging, he was tired of standing still, tired of lying down. "I'm less than two months old and I'm tired of living," he said. He walked out to the yard again.

"When I'm out here," he said, "there's no place to go but in. When I'm indoors, there's no place to go but out in the yard."

"That's where you're wrong, my friend, my friend," said a voice.

Wilbur looked through the fence and saw the goose standing there.

"You don't have to stay in that dirty-little dirty-little dirty-little yard," said the goose, who talked rather fast. "One of the boards is loose. Push on it, push-push-push on it, and come on out!"

"What?" said Wilbur. "Say it slower!"

"At-at-at, at the risk of repeating myself," said the goose, "I suggest that you come on out. It's wonderful out here."

"Did you say a board was loose?"

"That I did, that I did," said the goose.

Wilbur walked up to the fence and saw that the goose was right – one board was loose. He put his head down, shut his eyes, and pushed. The board gave way. In a minute he had squeezed through the fence and was standing in the long grass outside his yard. The goose chuckled.

"How does it feel to be free?" she asked.

"I like it," said Wilbur. "That is, I *guess* I like it."

Actually, Wilbur felt queer to be outside his fence, with nothing between him and the big world.

"Where do you think I'd better go?"

"Anywhere you like, anywhere you like," said the goose. "Go down through the orchard, root up the sod! Go down through the garden, dig up the radishes! Root up everything! Eat grass! Look for corn! Look for oats! Run all over! Skip and dance, jump and prance! Go down through the orchard and stroll in the woods! The world is a wonderful place when you're young."

"I can see that," replied Wilbur. He gave a jump in the air, twirled, ran a few steps, stopped, looked all round, sniffed the smells of afternoon, and then set off walking down through the orchard. Pausing in the shade of an apple tree, he put his strong snout into the ground and began pushing, digging, and rooting. He felt very happy. He had ploughed up quite a piece of ground before anyone noticed him. Mrs Zuckerman was the first to see him. She saw him from the kitchen window, and she immediately shouted for the men.

"Ho-*mer*!" she cried. "Pig's out! Lurvy! Pig's out! Homer! Lurvy! Pig's out. He's down there under that apple tree."

"Now the trouble starts," thought Wilbur. "Now I'll catch it."

The goose heard the racket and she, too, started hollering. "Run-run-run downhill, make for the woods, the woods!" she shouted to Wilbur. "They'll never-never-never catch you in the woods."

The cocker spaniel heard the commotion and he ran out from the barn to join in the chase. Mr Zuckerman heard, and he came out of the machine shed where he was mending a tool. Lurvy, the hired man, heard the noise and came up from the asparagus patch where he was pulling weeds. Everybody walked towards Wilbur and Wilbur didn't know what to do. The woods seemed a long way off, and anyway, he had never been down there in the woods and wasn't sure he would like it.

"Get round behind him, Lurvy," said Mr Zuckerman, "and drive him towards the barn! And take it easy – don't rush him! I'll go and get a bucket of slops."

The news of Wilbur's escape spread rapidly among the animals on the place. Whenever any creature broke loose on Zuckerman's farm, the event was of great interest to the others. The goose shouted to the nearest cow that Wilbur was free, and soon all the cows knew. Then one of the cows told one of the sheep, and soon all the sheep knew. The lambs learned about it from their mothers. The horses, in their stalls in the barn, pricked up their ears when they heard the goose hollering; and soon the horses had caught on to what was happening. "Wilbur's out," they said. Every animal stirred its head and became excited to know that one of its friends had got free and was no longer penned up or tied fast.

Wilbur didn't know what to do or which way to run. It seemed as though everybody was after him. "If this is what it's like to be free," he thought, "I believe I'd rather be penned up in my own yard."

The cocker spaniel was sneaking up on him from one side, Lurvy the hired man was sneaking up on him from the other side. Mrs Zuckerman stood ready to head him off if he started for the garden, and now Mr Zuckerman was coming down towards him carrying a pail. "This is really awful," thought Wilbur. "Why doesn't Fern come?" He began to cry.

The goose took command and began to give orders.

"Don't just stand there, Wilbur! Dodge about, dodge about!" cried the goose. "Skip around, run towards me, slip in and out, in and out, in and out! Make for the woods! Twist and turn!"

The cocker spaniel sprang for Wilbur's hind leg. Wilbur jumped and ran. Lurvy reached out and grabbed. Mrs Zuckerman screamed at Lurvy. The goose cheered for Wilbur. Wilbur dodged between Lurvy's legs. Lurvy missed Wilbur and grabbed the spaniel instead. "Nicely done, nicely done!" cried the goose. "Try it again, try it again."

"Run downhill!" suggested the cows.

"Run towards me!" yelled the gander.

"Run uphill!" cried the sheep.

"Turn and twist!" honked the goose.

"Jump and dance!" said the rooster.

"Look out for Lurvy!" called the cows.

"Look out for Zuckerman!" yelled the gander.

"Watch out for the dog!" cried the sheep.

"Listen to me, listen to me!" screamed the goose.

Poor Wilbur was dazed and frightened by this hullabaloo. He didn't like being the centre of all this fuss. He tried to follow the instructions his friends were giving him, but he couldn't run downhill and uphill at the same time, and he couldn't turn and twist when he was jumping and dancing, and he was crying so hard he could barely see anything that was happening. After all, Wilbur was a very young pig – not much more than a baby, really. He wished Fern were here to take him in her arms and comfort him. When he looked up and saw Mr Zuckerman standing quite close to him, holding a pail of warm slops, he felt relieved. He lifted his nose and sniffed. The smell was delicious – warm milk, potato skins, wheat middlings, toasted corn flakes, and a popover left from the Zuckermans' breakfast.

"Come, pig!" said Mr Zuckerman, tapping the pail. "Come, pig!"

Wilbur took a step towards the pail.

"No-no-no!" said the goose. "It's the old pail trick, Wilbur. Don't fall for it, don't fall for it! He's trying to lure you back into captivity-ivity. He's appealing to your stomach."

Wilbur didn't care. The food smelled appetizing. He tock another step towards the pail.

"Pig, pig!" said Mr Zuckerman in a kind

voice, and began walking slowly towards the barnyard, looking all about him innocently, as if he didn't know that a little white pig was following along behind him.

"You'll be sorry-sorry-sorry," called the goose.

Wilbur didn't care. He kept walking towards the pail of slops.

"You'll miss your freedom," honked the goose. "An hour of freedom is worth a barrel of slops."

Wilbur didn't care.

When Mr Zuckerman reached the pigpen, he climbed over the fence and poured the slops into the trough. Then he pulled the loose board away from the fence, so that there was a wide hole for Wilbur to walk through.

"Reconsider, reconsider!" cried the goose.

Wilbur paid no attention. He stepped through the fence into his yard. He walked to the trough and took a long drink of slops, sucking in the milk hungrily and chewing the popover. It was good to be home again.

While Wilbur ate, Lurvy fetched a hammer and some eight-penny nails and nailed the board in place. Then he and Mr Zuckerman leaned lazily on the fence and Mr Zuckerman scratched Wilbur's back with a stick.

"He's quite a pig," said Lurvy.

"Yes, he'll make a good pig," said Mr Zuckerman. Wilbur heard the words of praise. He felt the warm milk inside his stomach. He felt the pleasant rubbing of the stick along his itchy back. He felt peaceful and happy and sleepy. This had been a tiring afternoon. It was still only about four o'clock but Wilbur was ready for bed.

"I'm really too young to go out into the world alone," he thought as he lay down.

Coyote and the Mice

A story of the North American Indians

Retold by Gail Robinson and Douglas Hill

O ne day during a summer in the world's beginning when rain came only in the early season of the sun, Coyote was travelling across the prairie. The heat dried his tongue and lips until it seemed that they would crack like the hard-baked surface of the soil. So he felt great relief when dusk brought the coolness of a prairie evening, and when he came to a small creek with a trickle of water still in it. There he found a copse of birch, white poplar and willow trees, and there too was a shallow grassy dip in the ground, just big enough for his body, and still cupping within itself some of the warmth of the day.

So Coyote curled around and lay down in

that welcome bed, exhausted and ready for a long sleep. But the night was full of disturbance. He spent much of it sneezing mosquitoes away from his nose and listening to them whine spitefully around his ears. And he sneezed even more when a chill eastern breeze arose to wipe away the last of the warmth from the ground. But at last he drifted into a restless, fretful sleep, and managed even to stay in it while shivering under the silver-cold full moon that rose later to glare down onto his bed.

But then the moonlight brought out the worst disturbance of all. A horde of mice – Coyote felt there were hundreds – came running down to the creek, and skittered over Coyote's legs and body as if he were no more than a log lying in their path.

Angrily, but not fully awake, Coyote threshed about under their tiny scratching paws and flailed with his legs. "Can you not find another path?" he growled, then rolled over to resume his sleep.

For a long few moments there was stillness and silence around him, as if the mice had mysteriously vanished. Then through his hazy, weary half-sleep Coyote heard all the mouse voices raised in a high, shrill crying – louder than the whine of mosquitoes, but just as maddening.

"Be quiet!" Coyote grumbled from his sleep. "Go and do your singing somewhere else!" And he kicked out again with his legs into the grass around him, and rolled over again hoping to find a more comfortable position that would take him down into the deeper sleep he craved.

But instead he was brought fully awake, for the high-pitched keening rose even more loudly, until it seemed to scrape at his very eardrums.

"Stop that noise!" shouted Coyote, and rose to his feet in rage.

At once he saw the reason for the shrill crying sound. All around him in the grassy hollow where he had made his bed lay the tiny bodies of dead mice – killed by the threshing and rolling and kicking that he had done, trying to preserve his restless sleep. And the high keening was the noise of grief, being made by the many dozens of living mice weeping among their dead.

Coyote felt a small bitter tendril of guilt creep within his belly, at the sight of the slaughter and pain he had caused. But guilt is an uncomfortable feeling, and Coyote quickly hid it from himself. He hid it by covering it up, with anger and with blame.

"Be off!" he shouted. "None of this would have happened had you not come along to interrupt my sleep! Now get away, and disturb me no more!"

And he lunged towards the mice, with a snarl and a flash of teeth, till they scrambled away for safety.

In the quiet that the mice left behind them, Coyote once again curled himself into the shallow hole – well away from the tiny still bodies – and closed his eyes, gritty with lack of sleep.

Full daylight and the risen sun were penetrating the leaves of the copse by the time he awakened. And once again he was brought out of his sleep by the shrill cries of mice. But this time the cries filled Coyote with fear, not anger. They were the sort of cries made by creatures of the wilderness when they sense the coming of great terror – fire or flood or windstorm.

Coyote leaped up, hardly noticing that some time in the night the dead mice had been silently removed from the hollow. "What is it?" he cried. "What is happening?"

"Run, Coyote! Hide!" shouted the mice, rushing towards him. "A mighty hailstorm is sweeping across the land, with ice-stones the size of your head falling to crush any living thing beneath them! We must all hide!"

"But you have only to creep into your holes and burrows to be safe," cried Coyote, almost weeping with fear. "What shall I do? Where can I hide?"

"We are not as safe as you think," said one of the older mice. "We cannot all get into our burrows at once – there are too many of us. We are never all together in our nests at the same time, because some of us are guarding the entrances, and many others are out gathering food. So most of us here will have to stay above ground during the storm."

"But how will you protect yourselves? How will I protect myself?" whimpered Coyote.

"We have a way," said another mouse. "We climb into bags of especially tough buffalo hide, then with ropes we pull ourselves up into the trees where the boughs and leaves are extra protection."

"What a clever idea," said Coyote. "I hope you have a hide-bag big enough for me?"

"But why should we help you," said several mice, "when you cruelly and carelessly killed so many of us during the night, without showing any sympathy?"

With those words, that small tendril of guilt inside Coyote grew suddenly larger, strengthened by his fear. Tears sprang from his eyes as he fell on his knees before the mice, babbling apologies, begging forgiveness, praying that they would help him now in spite of what had happened the night before.

"You would not let the storm kill me," he wept, "because of something I did while I was half asleep and not paying proper attention?"

At that, a grandmotherly mouse stepped forward. "We could say that you *should* have been paying attention, to the lives of other creatures. But let that now all be past. Here is a bag that will hold you. Into it quickly, now, for the sky is darkening."

So it was, as Coyote saw with a fearful glance upwards. Of course, it was the time of year, as he knew, when the north wind often blew heavy low clouds over the plain. But Coyote did not stop to think too long about clouds. He watched the mice scrambling into their bags, and the darting swiftness of their movements infected him with a new panic. Hastily he climbed into his own bag, first throwing the rope from the bag's drawstring up over a tree branch, as he had seen the mice do. Then, his arms extended out of the neck of the bag, he pulled himself up until he was swinging in mid-air. Finally he knotted the other end of the rope on to the drawstring and pulled his arms into the bag, while his own weight drew the neck of the bag tightly closed.

Then he waited, inside the stifling bag. The rough and dusty hair of the hide had been turned inwards, and as he tried to find a comfortable position his nose became irritated and his eyes began to run. Worse still, his movements caused the bag to swing, and the springiness of the branch it was tied to kept up a steady rocking, lurching motion so that Coyote began to feel decidedly sick.

But he curled up in a tight ball, telling himself that any discomfort and hardship was better than being killed by a downpour of enormous hailstones. And just as that thought crossed his mind, a gust of wind swung the bag even more strongly, and he heard the shrieking of the mice.

"Here comes the hail! Here comes the hail!"

And as he heard it, he felt a sharp impact and a blazing pain on his side – and another blow almost at the same time on a knee – and another agonizing blow on his lower back – and more blows, and bruising pains, all over his back and bottom and legs and shoulders and head; any place that was touching the hide – and more, and more . . .

Some little distance from the copse of trees

where Coyote was in such pain, a group of the People walked quietly together, talking of many things. Some had looked up to notice that the wind was clearing away the low, churning bank of black clouds that had blown up – and that wide stretches of blue sky were beginning to appear. As they walked, the People suddenly became aware of a loud shrieking and howling that was coming from a small stand of trees nearby.

They hurried over to find out the cause of the noise. When they reached the copse, they stood silent with amazement.

They saw a large, bulging bag of buffalo hide suspended from the branch of a tree. And beneath it they saw dozens upon dozens of mice, pelting the bag with a barrage of sharp stones which other mice were carrying up from the nearby creek-bed.

"Ow, ow, owooooo!" howled the bag, in the unmistakable voice of Coyote.

"Oh, ow, the pain, help, oh!" shouted the mice, not pausing in their hurling of stones. "The hail is getting worse, the hailstones are getting bigger!"

"They are, they are!" wailed Coyote. "Ow, owooo!"

And so they were, for the mice were now gathering and flinging the largest stones they could find, and so many of them that they rattled against the hide-bag and its bruised contents with the speed of real hail.

At this point Quail, who had a tender heart and could not bear any form of cruelty, stepped from the watching group of the People.

"Why are you doing this?" she asked one of the mice, who was gathering stones nearby. "You will kill him."

In reply the mouse led Quail deeper into the copse of trees, and pointed out the bodies of her two children, lying among the other mice that had died the night before.

"They died because Coyote was careless and indifferent to others," said the mouse. "We do not intend to kill him – only to teach him a lesson about suffering, about paying attention to other creatures. There would be no point in killing him, for then there would be no learning.

In a short while the cries and howls from the hide-bag began to grow weaker, and at a sign from one of their elders the mice put down their last stones and lowered the bag out of the tree. They pulled the drawstring open, and there lay Coyote – unable to move, dreadfully battered, covered with lumps and bruises. At first he could not even see, for swellings around his eyes had squeezed them shut. But the mice bathed his head and face in sweet balsam water, and finally he managed to raise an eyelid and look around him.

He saw the People, standing beyond the mice, watching as quietly as the shadows of the trees behind them. He saw the mice, also standing silently, looking altogether healthy and unaffected by any hailstorm. He saw the sky, clear blue now, entirely free of clouds. He saw the dry, dry ground.

But, most vividly, he saw the huge pile of stones, large and small, strewn beneath and around the tree where he had hung as helpless as a bird's nest.

Coyote stared foolishly at all these sights. He could see exactly what had happened. And, deep within himself, where that tendril of guilt coiled and grew, he knew exactly why it had happened.

Slowly, dazedly, with every sore place on his body crying out in pain, he struggled to his feet.

"Why," he said, "you have tricked me half to death."

The Very Greedy Monster

John Cunliffe

Once there was a Monster. He lived far away on an island. He was very big, and very strong, and very greedy. He was so big, and so strong, that none of the other creatures could fight him. He was so greedy, that wanting something and getting it, were the same thing to him. So he grew bigger, and stronger, and greedier, with each day that passed. He had a wonderful life. He ate what he liked. He did what he liked. He played with whoever he liked; the other animals were so afraid of him, that if he shouted, "Come and play with me!" they just had to. But to be friends with Monster, or to play with him, was just as dangerous as fighting him, as you will see.

One day, Monster was playing at racing along the beach with three antelopes. Now antelopes can run very fast, but they ran slowly, to let Monster win. They knew he would be angry if he didn't win. So the first race, the second race, and the third race, Monster won easily. This made him proud, and he strutted about, bellowing, "See what a fine Monster I am! I can race you silly antelopes, easy as easy. Pooh, I could race you backwards!"

This was too much for Tappo, the youngest of the antelopes. "That's not *fair!*" he shouted. "Give us one more race and we'll show you."

"Hush. Hush," said the other antelopes, trembling with fear.

"I'll race you any day," said Monster. "Backwards, forwards, upside-down, legs tied together, any way you like!"

"We challenge you to an ordinary forwards race," said Tappo, refusing to be hushed.

"Very well," said Monster. "One, two . . ." he began counting, then he was off before the antelopes, and shouting over his shoulder, "three, GO!" Now the antelopes were so angry at this cheating, that this time they ran as fast as they could. Their legs moved at such speed that they were just a blur. They soon caught up with Monster, who was wallowing along in the sand. Then they passed him and reached the palm-tree winning-post well ahead of him.

"Now who's the winner?" said Tappo.

"I am," said Monster, "because you cheated."

"*We* cheated? You're the one who cheated," said Tappo.

"I'm not arguing," said Monster. Then he opened his wide mouth, and gobbled up the three antelopes, GULP, just like that. "I'm the winner," he said, and there was no answer.

Another day, Monster was playing with some giraffes. There was an argument about who had the longest neck.

"Anyone can see," said one giraffe, "that our necks are the longest. No animal in the world has a neck as long as ours. It's our special point of beauty. You have a nice neck, Monster, but it's quite short."

"I'm not arguing," said the Monster. Then he opened wide his enormous mouth, and gobbled up the giraffes, all six of them, GULP, just like that.

"My neck is the longest," he said and there was no answer.

Things became worse and worse. Sooner or later, Monster quarrelled with everyone. He gobbled up all the monkeys, the hippopotami, the ostriches, the elephants, the snakes, the lizards, the lions, the tigers and the baboons.

Now Mother Monster and Father Monster noticed what was happening, and they didn't like it at all.

"You shouldn't gobble up all your play-mates," said Mother Monster, "even if you are a monster. Even monsters need someone to play with, and someone to talk to."

"Nonsense," said Monster.

"Don't talk to me like that," said Mother Monster, "or I'll have to give you a smack." (She had not noticed how big her Monster had grown.)

Monster just said, "Oh no you won't give me a smack. And I'm not arguing with you, either." Then he opened his terrible mouth and gobbled up Mother Monster, GULP, just like that.

"I'll gobble who I like," he said, and there was no answer.

But Father Monster saw what had happened and he came running to give Monster the first and best smacking of his life.

"Oh no you don't," said Monster, and he opened his cavelike mouth, and gobbled up Father Monster, GULP, just like that.

"I'll do just what I like," he said. "I'll gobble up who I like, when I like, *so there*," and there was no reply.

The next day, Monster gobbled up all the crocodiles, the alligators, the birds, the gorillas, the leopards, the cheetahs, the sloths and the bears. By the end of the week, he had gobbled up every creature on his island.

"Now I'm the master of all the world!" he shouted. There was no reply. "I'm the strongest, the fastest, the best, of all creatures," he bellowed. There was no reply. Monster went to sleep, feeling well pleased with himself.

Next morning, forgetting what he had done, Monster woke up, and bellowed, "Come and play with me!" There was no reply. Louder still he shouted. "Come and play with me! I want someone to play with! Come out at once, or I'll gobble you all up!" Silence. Nothing moved. Then, "Oh," he said. "Oh, dear, I had quite forgotten. I *have* gobbled you up. All of you. Who will I play with now?"

Suddenly, Monster felt a deep sadness inside him. For the first time in his life, he began to cry. He cried all day and cried himself to sleep when night came again.

As the days went by, Monster became thinner and thinner. He was too sad to eat, too sad to play, too sad to live.

"What's the use of being the only creature alive in all the world?" he said. "I wish I could gobble myself up." But that was one thing he could not gobble up. So he lay down on the beach, and ate nothing at all, and hoped he would soon die of hunger.

What Monster did not know was that his island was not the whole world at all, but only a tiny part of it. There were many other lands out of sight across the sea, all of them teeming with animals. So Monster was surprised when, as he lay upon the beach too weak to move, a dolphin came swimming up to him.

"Hello, what's wrong with you?" asked Dolphin. "What a funny beast you are. Are you ill? Can I help?"

"You must be a dream," said Monster, weakly. "I've eaten everybody in all the world."

"You look very thin on it," said the dolphin. "Anyway, you haven't eaten me, or the whales, or the fish, or the porpoises, I've just seen millions of them. There's more to the world than this little island, you know. Much more. There are hundreds of islands, most of them bigger than this one, and bigger places, too."

Then the dolphin told Monster all about the world and Monster began to cheer up. He told the dolphin his story, and why he was so lonely that he wanted to die.

So the dolphin said, "I'll tell you what I'll do. I'll be your friend! But you must promise not to gobble me up, whatever happens."

"Oh, I promise. I promise," said Monster. "I'll never gobble anyone up again. I'll eat coconuts, and leaves, and oranges."

He kept his promise and the dolphin came to see him each day. He told Monster stories about the world and played with him in the shallow water. As the days passed, Monster grew slowly stronger. Now that he had a friend, he no longer wanted to die, and he had come to like living on fruits, and leaves, and the roots he dug from the ground.

One day, he said to the dolphin, "If you know anyone who would like to come and live here, it would be quite safe for them, now."

"I'll pass the word round," said the Dolphin.

So, quite soon, a whole family of alligators arrived on Monster's island and they quickly made friends. Then some crocodiles came, and some swimming snakes. A flock of birds flying over, came down to rest, and stayed to live on the island. Little by little, life came back to the island. Monster made friends with every creature, and there was no one more kind and gentle than he. He played with the little crocodiles, and let them climb over his back. He allowed the little alligators to pull his tail and tweak his toes in fun. Monster was happy again. But all the animals said, "How strange it is that such a big strong animal should be so kind and gentle."

The dolphin smiled to himself, when he heard this, but he kept Monster's secret, and said never a word about it.

Rabbit and Tiger

A Story from South America

Grace Hallworth

Early one morning, Tiger was taking a walk through the forest when she heard someone making a great noise. Tiger crept forward to see who it was, and saw Konehu the rabbit pulling vines off a tree.

Tiger was surprised, for it was a strange thing to see Konehu working hard so early in the day.

"Ho Konehu!" called Tiger. "What are you doing up so early?"

"Tiger, you don't know that a big storm is coming and anyone who is not tied to a tree will be blown away?" enquired Konehu.

Of course Tiger was very worried when she heard this and begged Konehu to tie her tight to a tree.

213

But Konehu said, "Look Tiger, the storm will soon be here. I can't stop to bind you. Why not take these vines and bind yourself, as I shall do?"

Tiger knew that she would not be able to bind herself firmly enough, so she flattered Konehu with much sweet talk:

"You are small, Konehu, but you are so much cleverer than me in matters of this kind. I know that if you bind me, no matter how hard the wind blows, I shall be safe."

So Konehu bound Tiger tight, tight to a tree with the vines.

Then he went a little way, and began to pull more vines off another tree! Tiger heard, and chuckled to herself,

"How stupid Konehu is to think that he can bind himself to a tree. Why, the wind will blow him away at the first strong gust!"

But Konehu was only pretending. Soon he crept through the trees and went home.

Tiger waited all night for the storm to begin, but when the next day dawned clear and bright, Tiger remembered that Konehu was always playing tricks. She tried to loosen the vines that bound her, but they were firm and secure.

At midday the animals of the forest began to make their way down to the river.

First came Goat, with long sharp horns. Tiger greeted him: "Goat, please untie these vines that bind me fast, lest I die of hunger and thirst."

But Goat was afraid that Tiger was so hungry that she would eat him up, so he said:

"Tiger, I'll just go and sharpen my horns to loosen the knots." And Goat hurried away.

When some time had gone by and Goat did not return, Tiger again tried to bite through the vines to loosen them, but they were green and strong. Tiger would have lost every tooth before she loosened one knot.

Then came Mongoose with his sharp teeth. He was slily slinking past and looking for his enemy Snake.

Tiger called out to Mongoose, "Brer Mongoose, please untie these knots and set me free, lest I die of hunger and thirst."

Mongoose whispered, "I'll be back, Tiger, as soon as I have sharpened my teeth." And he slid away under the rotting leaves in the forest.

Soon it was late afternoon, and Tiger's throat was so dry that she could hardly raise her voice when Corbeau flew by. Corbeau's thick black feathers were glossy, for she had feasted well and was on her way to the river.

Tiger called, "Oh, my friend Corbeau, for pity's sake loosen my cords, or I shall die of hunger and thirst."

Tiger looked so weak and thin that Corbeau felt sorry for her. With her sharp beak, Corbeau untied the knots and loosened the vines and set Tiger free.

And that is why, to this day, Tiger never eats all that she kills but leaves something behind for Corbeau to eat.

Now Tiger was determined to kill Konehu the rabbit, so day after day she roamed the forest looking for him.

One day she spotted the rabbit high, high up on a rock gazing into the forest pool below. The yellow sun overhead, reflected in the water, looked like a golden ball.

"Konehu, Konehu, I am coming to kill you!" roared Tiger.

"Oh Tiger, you are just in time to witness a wonderful sight," said Konehu.

Tiger climbed right up to the rock where Konehu sat.

"What are you looking at?" asked Tiger.

"See that golden ball in the pool?" said Konehu. "If only we could get it out we would be richer than the King."

Tiger looked down at the golden ball. It was so bright that it lit up the water in the pool.

"Konehu" she said, "you are too small to lift such a large ball. Let me go in and bring it up for you."

Tiger intended to run off with the gold and keep it all for herself.

"Very well," said Konehu, "but when you get it, hold it fast. Don't let it slip from you or it will go deeper."

Quickly Tiger dived into the pool, but she soon came up spluttering and snorting. She had not found the gold.

Konehu called to her:

*"Tiger my friend, be brave, be bold.
Go deep and deep to find the gold."*

So once more Tiger dived down, down into the pool, into the cool water, and once more Tiger rose up puffing and blowing so hard that she sprayed Konehu where he sat high up on the rock.

Tiger was ready to give up the search, but Konehu shouted:

*"Tiger, you must be brave and bold.
Go deeper still to find the gold."*

This time Tiger dived deep, deep, so deep that she did not come up again.

Some say she was drowned. Others say she went so deep that she came out on the other side of the world in India, where she lives to this day.

But whichever story is true, Konehu is still laughing at how he made Tiger believe that the sun's reflection was a golden ball.

ACKNOWLEDGEMENTS

The publishers wish to thank the following for permission to reproduce copyright material. All possible care has been taken to trace the ownership of every story included and to make full acknowledgements for its use. If any errors have accidentally occurred, they will be corrected in subsequent editions, provided notification is sent to the publishers.

Dick King-Smith: 'Woolly' from *Animal Stories*, by Dick King-Smith; first published by Penguin Books Ltd, 1997. Copyright © Fox Busters Ltd, 1997. Reproduced by permission of A. P. Watt Ltd on behalf of Fox Busters Ltd

Colin Thompson: 'Sid the Mosquito' from *Sid the Mosquito*, by Colin Thompson; first published by Knight Books, 1993. Copyright © Colin Thompson, 1991, 1993. Reproduced by permission of Hodder and Stoughton Ltd

Nora Clarke: 'Billy Bear's Stumpy Tail' from *A Treasury of Animal Stories*, chosen by Jane Olliver. Copyright © Grisewood & Demsey Ltd, 1991. Reproduced by permission of Larousse Plc

Michael Morpurgo: 'The Fourth Life of Montezuma' from *Nine Lives of Montezuma*; first published by Heinemann, 1980. Copyright © Kaye & Ward Ltd, 1980. Reproduced by permission of Reed Consumer Books Ltd

Michael Bond: 'Olga's Day Off' from *The Tales of Olga da Polga*, by Michael Bond; first published by Penguin Books Ltd. Copyright © Michael Bond, 1971. Reproduced by permission of The Agency (London) Ltd

Rudyard Kipling: 'The Elephant's Child' (excluding final poem) from *Just So Stories*, by Rudyard Kipling; first published by Macmillan, 1902. Reproduced by permission of A.P.Watt on behalf of The National Trust

David Henry Wilson: 'Yucky Ducky' from *Yucky Ducky*, by David Henry Wilson; first published by J. M. Dent & Sons Ltd, 1988. Copyright © David Henry Wilson, 1988. Reproduced by permission of The Agency (London) Ltd

Dorothy Cottrell: 'Chut the Kangaroo' from *Pet Stories for Children*, edited by Sara and Stephen Corrin. Copyright © Faber and Faber Ltd, 1985

John Yeoman: 'How the Turtle Got His Shell' from *The Singing Tortoise and Other Animal Folk Tales*, by John Yeoman; first published by Victor Gollancz/Hamish Hamilton. Copyright © John Yeoman, 1993. Reproduced by permission of Penguin Books Ltd on behalf of the author

ACKNOWLEDGEMENTS

Philippa Pearce: 'Life With Tilly' from *A Dog So Small*, by Philippa Pearce; first published by Longman Young Books, Penguin Children's Books, 1962. Copyright © Philippa Pearce, 1962. Reproduced by permission of Penguin Books Ltd

Ted Hughes: 'How the Cat Became' from *How the Whale Became and Other Stories*, by Ted Hughes. Reproduced by permission of Faber and Faber Ltd

Gordon Snell: 'Wandering Prince' from *Wild and Free*, chosen by Wendy Cooling; first published by Orion Children's Books, 1997 and reproduced by permission of Orion Publishing Group Ltd

Rose Fyleman: 'The Crocodile and the Monkey' from *Folk Tales from Many Lands* first published by Faber & Faber Ltd. Reproduced by permission of The Society of Authors

E. B. White: 'Escape' from *Charlotte's Web* by E. B. White; first published by Hamish Hamilton Children's Books, 1952. Copyright © E. B. White, 1952, renewed copyright © E. B. White, 1980. Reproduced by permission of Frederick Warne & Co and HarperCollins Publishers Inc

Gail Robinson and Douglas Hill: 'Coyote and the Mice' from *Coyote the Trickster* retold by Gail Robinson and Douglas Hill; first published by Chatto & Windus, 1975 and reproduced by permission of Watson, Little Ltd

John Cunliffe: 'The Very Greedy Monster' from *Dragon Stories* by John Cunliffe; first published by Andre Deutsch Children's Books, an imprint of Scholastic Ltd, 1973. Copyright © John Cunliffe, 1973. Reproduced by permission of Scholastic Ltd

Grace Hallworth, 'Rabbit and Tiger' from *Cric Crac*, by Grace Hallworth; first published by William Heinemann Ltd. Reproduced by permission of Reed Consumer Books Ltd

Books in this series available from Macmillan

The prices shown below are correct at the time of going to press.
However, Macmillan Publishers reserves the right to show new retail
prices on covers which may differ from those previously advertised.

Adventure Stories for Five Year Olds	0 330 39137 2	£4.99
Animal Stories for Five Year Olds	0 330 39125 9	£4.99
Bedtime Stories for Five Year Olds	0 330 48366 8	£4.99
Funny Stories for Five Year Olds	0 330 39124 0	£4.99
Magical Stories for Five Year Olds	0 330 39122 4	£4.99
Adventure Stories for Six Year Olds	0 330 39138 0	£4.99
Animal Stories for Six Year Olds	0 330 36859 1	£4.99
Bedtime Stories for Six Year Olds	0 330 48368 4	£4.99
Funny Stories for Six Year Olds	0 330 36857 5	£4.99
Magical Stories for Six Year Olds	0 330 36858 3	£4.99
Adventure Stories for Seven Year Olds	0 330 39139 9	£4.99
Animal Stories for Seven Year Olds	0 330 35494 9	£4.99
Funny Stories for Seven Year Olds	0 330 34945 7	£4.99
Scary Stories for Seven Year Olds	0 330 34943 0	£4.99
School Stories for Seven Year Olds	0 330 48378 1	£4.99
Adventure Stories for Eight Year Olds	0 330 39140 2	£4.99
Animal Stories for Eight Year Olds	0 330 35495 7	£4.99
Funny Stories for Eight Year Olds	0 330 34946 5	£4.99
Scary Stories for Eight Year Olds	0 330 34944 9	£4.99
School Stories for Eight Year Olds	0 330 48379 X	£4.99
Adventure Stories for Nine Year Olds	0 330 39141 0	£4.99
Animal Stories for Nine Year Olds	0 330 37493 1	£4.99
Funny Stories for Nine Year Olds	0 330 37491 5	£4.99
Revolting Stories for Nine Year Olds	0 330 48370 6	£4.99
Scary Stories for Nine Year Olds	0 330 37492 3	£4.99
Adventure Stories for Ten Year Olds	0 330 39142 9	£4.99
Animal Stories for Ten Year Olds	0 330 39128 3	£4.99
Funny Stories for Ten Year Olds	0 330 39127 5	£4.99
Revolting Stories for Ten Year Olds	0 330 48372 2	£4.99
Scary Stories for Ten Year Olds	0 330 39126 7	£4.99

All Pan Macmillan titles can be ordered from our website,
www.panmacmillan.com, or from your local bookshop
and are also available by post from:
Bookpost
PO Box 29, Douglas, Isle of Man IM99 1BQ

Credit cards accepted. For details:
Telephone: +44(0)1624 677237
Fax: +44(0)1624 670923
Email: bookshop@enterprise.net
www.bookpost.co.uk

Free postage and packing in the UK.